W9-CAP-835

APR -- 2012

make it stay

Also by Joan Frank

In Envy Country

The Great Far Away

Miss Kansas City

Boys Keep Being Born

make it
stay

joan frank

The Permanent Press
Sag Harbor, NY 11963

For information, address:
  The Permanent Press
  4170 Noyac Road
  Sag Harbor, NY 11963
  www.thepermanentpress.com

Library of Congress Cataloging-in-Publication Data

Frank, Joan–
    Make it stay / Joan Frank.
        pages cm
    ISBN 978-1-57962-227-5
        1. Married people—Fiction. 2. Male friendship—Fiction.
    3. Psychological fiction. I. Title.

PS3606.R38M35 2012
813'.6—dc23   2011048286

Printed in the United States of America.

For Bob, always

Acknowledgments

I am grateful to Joan Acocella (and her publisher Alfred A. Knopf, a division of Random House, Inc.), for permission to excerpt a line from her essay collection *Twenty-Eight Artists and Two Saints*; to Kay Ryan, for permission to allude to her title poem from *The Niagara River*; to Marty and Judith Shepard, who stepped forward to say yes; to Jeffrey Levine, for seconding that motion; to Ianthe Brautigan, whose wisdom and loyalty keep me afloat; to friends and family for putting up with me—and to Bob Duxbury, for a lifetime's love and forbearance.

*I*t is a species of sentimentality to believe that the end of something tells the truth about it.

—JOAN ACOCELLA
Twenty-Eight Artists and Two Saints

- I -

The cooking? An act of aggression, against an industrially grim childhood. It took Neil years, for instance, to be able to face cabbage again. (Glasgow school kids groaned to look at the stuff—hauled to the cafeteria in a vat, stinking, when the enormous lid was lifted away, like dirty laundry.) But when at last he did face it, he knew to sauté the raw leaves very quickly in olive oil, turning them bright green. Salt, pepper, sprinkle of red chili flakes. The Scot in him craved pub culture, but few could afford to go out, those years. So Neil gave dinners, more soup kitchen at first than pressed linen. Two pots of spaghetti, a pan of half-burnt garlic bread. He'd scrape the black off. "Eh, get it down ye." Guests stood in line for helpings, he tells me. They manifested at the appointed time, like parachutists fallen in together. Then I became part of it. In good weather we sat on the porch or in the backyard on folding chairs, balancing plates, plastic cups of wine, beer. Over years Neil aimed higher: mussels, cassoulet, duck. Big, peasant portions. You thought of Brueghel. Have we resembled Brueghel people, round and ribald, feasting on brined turkey and wine-braised ribs and gorgonzola polenta?

Gangly Neil's the exemption, burns calories thinking. Or so he claims, laughing, pleased he's held off this earmark of age—though we both know it's no feat of will on his part, only genetic grace. I've learned to live with that. Learned to live with him reading cookbooks beside me in bed at night, stork-legs crossed, pointing at the photos while I correct (try to correct) page proofs.

"D'you like that? Or how about that?"

"Oooh, I like that. And that. And oh, oh—that."

Food porn, they call it now. By 2005 I had let him convince me to move in.

A risk, at our ages. We'd dated, commuting, a few years. The house was his, so I gave up my city apartment. Rough on me. I remember weeping as I drove the U-Haul packed with my things—meager as twigs they seemed—across Golden Gate Bridge that baking August afternoon, pastel skyline streaming along-side in the sun. I was already forty, had lived alone a dozen years. But at what age does one call a total moratorium on risk? And how could I resist when Neil, reading my tears, took me by the shoulders, his voice going higher:

"If you hate it, we'll find another house and move!"

We didn't move.

We put in carpets. Neil repainted—the same month, August—sweating, grunting, kerchief knotted over his skull like a pirate. I came to love the wide, leafy streets, their cut-grass scent, soundtrack of birdsong; the wine country hills, redwood groves. Against ridiculous odds we became a thing: part him, part me. All I know is it had to do with time. Of course there were crises, shouting. I still remember moments that felt like freefall, sick at heart, when the sky lowered and everything turned the color of metal. But time, that solvent like no other, has almost erased these. Now it feels as though we've formed a kind of freight-bearing raft, best bits of ourselves lashed together to become seaworthy. Now and again, even this late, a leak spritzes open; we caulk it. Yes, both of us would have scorned such terms once. Bourgeois, we'd have sneered. Each of us had meant to live a billion times more boldly. Didn't everyone?

Time. Confederate and trickster. What I'm remembering happened more years ago than I can myself account for.

"Next onion, please."

Like a surgical nurse I hand him another, which I've shucked of its pink-gold skin. Droplets of white, north and south. Whick whack.

Here we are, beginning.

He likes, always, to try recipes. Well, to perfect them. Tonight's will be lamb with baby red potatoes, garlic, rosemary. Trifle for dessert. From my station at the sink I watch him whirl, sautéing croutons, mashing garlic—aromas crazy-making. I'll have to scrub the cutting board. Mike and Tilda have agreed to come, despite the difficulty. Tilda says it's good for Mike, getting out. Neil (crushing a clove, palm's heel against the flat of his knife) says it gives Tilda a break.

How I wish I could feel so easy about it.

"Remind me again," I press him.

*I*t was Neil who first knew them. Long ago, he claims it feels—says the 70s seem ancient now. In 1974 Neil was nineteen, Mike twenty-four. Neil worked in the Legal Aid office two doors down from Mike's aquarium shop. *Finny Business*: Mike always thought the name brilliantly hilarious; that part of him never changed. How he made any kind of living at the place, no one could figure. A dusty town Mira Flores was then, according to Neil; many streets still unpaved. Smells of firs, wisteria, jasmine in summer. Quiet like you don't find now. Light so clean you could taste it, and no one locked their doors. Someone said that in those years you could shoot a gun down the middle of the street and never hit a thing. People born here believed the town floated, Brigadoon-like, outside conventional space and time. A twinkling twirling sphere, perpetual, self-contained.

For a while, it must have seemed that way.

Each morning Mike leaned in his shop's open doorway, smoking—he smoked the way he did everything else, with calm abandon—eyeing the street, blinding passersby with his grin. Mike seemed to know everyone. God knew it was impossible not to notice him. That laugh alone: a thundercrack. It scared the unwary, made them jump and look around. Neil claimed the sound penetrated the glass doors of the Legal Aid lobby. The laugh, the bad puns, the jolly giant physique, strawberry beard—the BMW motorcycle, called Black Beast. Later, the bald head. Cartoon, people joked. Impossible corn, direct from central casting. The brawn, the boom, the Big Daddyness: *so over*, as the young now pitilessly say. But back then it impressed people. I suppose that is part of the paradox.

Mike's care of his fish, Neil says, was tender. Neil slipped over to the store every lunch hour, just to check it out. Inside was dark and cool; glass tanks of different sizes bubbled, their algae smell twisting up your nostrils, yeasty, an acrid overlay of chemicals, like fertilizer. Tank facades mirrored white daylight till you faced them head-on, when they revealed a series of clear, rippling worlds bejeweled with living exotica. Freshwater and marine. From the glass catfish—transparent wraiths whose backlit spines and guts made a 3-D anatomical display—to the dull but demanding piranhas (isolated, of course, like other attack-minded breeds). Soot-colored mollies, clownfish. One silvery blink called a topsword guppy—peer at it closehand, you saw it was painted with bright circles of red, green, yellow, like a Picasso print. Harlequins, discus, swordtail. The names were quirky, the appearances surpassing. Zebra fish, pencil fish, pike tops. Siamese fighters, their diaphanous fantails orange and blue like floor ruffles on evening gowns. Schools of cardinal tetra: neon-crimson streaks in perfect spatial unison. The tetra always drew a crowd—their illusion that of a single, shape-shifting, electrified thing zipping about. Mike had studied marine biology—no degree, but he lived at the library—between high school and joining the Navy, at nineteen. Though he'd lucked out with a low draft lottery number, he enlisted for an eighteen-month tour (serving as his ship's newspaper reporter, which spared him Vietnam combat), and had just completed it when his father died, at sixty, of a stroke. That was 1971. His mother apportioned some of the life insurance to her only child: that's how Mike could set up his store. He flew west to visit a Navy chum who'd been staying with family in Mira Flores. The town delighted him; warmer and dryer all year than any of his New England experience, blazing with multicolored flowers and trees, peaceful, pretty. Not least, the Northern California coastline was only a forty-minute drive.

"This is it," Mike told Neil boastfully, when they began talking. "This is your last stop. You'll never want to leave."

His authority fairly clubbed you. Not just the shelves behind the register packed with titles, *Dictionary of Tropical Fish*, *Breeding in Captivity*, *The Nitrogen Cycle*, or the milk crates of *Tropical Fish Hobbyist* stacked by date: Mike buttonholed anyone who wandered in. Despite his circus strongman looks there was also in his manner something of the cracker-barrel sage, the type who once shod horses, dispensed aspirin and penny candy, thrust a tumbler of homebrew into your hand—color of dark tea, laceratingly alcoholic and rich as jam.

"Y'know," he'd rumble from behind them, startling customers, "Fish have been around a little longer than we have—two hundred fifty million years." People would back out of the store, nodding. The rudest shrugged and walked off. Mike took up his *récit* unfazed, with the next innocent browser. Neil, fascinated, watched this happen again and again. Since the days he'd squatted, a skinny kid, beside Cape Cod tide pools, Mike had revered water life. No detail too small. Take the false eye (he'd begin) on the rear dorsal fin of the marine betta. The fish resembles an owl's wing, its real face invisible. Predators bite toward the eye, to avoid getting scales and spines stuck in their throats. But if they strike at the false eye of the betta (here Mike's own brown-black eyes sparkled), "they'll only get a mouthful of finnage." He quoted from his *Tropical Fish Identifier* as from a beloved fairy tale. "And the betta will regrow its fin, and live to fight another day." Neil found himself dawdling in the store after lunch, entertained by Mike's spiel. He didn't care a damn about the fish, then or now—but couldn't help marvel at this man who resembled a bouncer at a strip club, tending his aquatic pets like a monk.

In those days, when he had no one else yet to pay for, Mike left Finny Business every year for a week or two in the care of a young assistant, and traveled half the world to dive for his rarest wares—the Marquesas, Tuamotus—air-freighting the specimens back. In 1976 Neil flew to Tahiti for a couple of weeks to visit Mike a few days. I've made him tell me the story more than once. He'd finagled reduced airfare by waiting standby for a flight chartered by a soccer team. (This resourcefulness did not surprise me. Neil emigrated to our vineyard town aiming to pass the California bar, interning at Legal Aid. He meant to practice here, and Scottish law did not transfer.) Funny, thinking of the young Neil. Thinner, paler. Kinky ginger hair in an Afro—Brits say ginger instead of red. There are so many kinds of red hair, some more pleasing than others. Neil's is a deep mercurochrome, with caramel mixed in. Tall. Spectacles. If you know the Irish actor Stephen Rea, that face is Neil's, including the funny, squared-off nose. A gentle, sad expression, as if all the world's problems swirled inside him and he's bitterly sorry he's not yet been able to fix them. I can see him waiting alone in the splintering boat, chin in hand like some bewildered schoolmaster after Mike heaved himself over the edge.

That wait frightened Neil. He'd hoped, after emigrating, never to have anything more to do with cold water than drink a glass of it. Not that Polynesian water was cold, of course. It was perfection, cool, jewel-blue. But that glittering afternoon, after Mike had maneuvered his craft through the shallows (a quarter-mile of coral edged the island like lace trim) and turned off his engine, the water became another thing. Razor blue, so brilliant to gaze on, Neil said, you felt the pupils of your eyes contract. When you looked down into it, the blue went black. The moist air smelled of salt, copra, Monoi Tiare, the gardenia-coconut oil women smeared on their hair and skin—no one having the mistiest notions then of words like *carcinoma* or *ozone hole*—and something more, a faint but pervasive stink, a sweetish rotting. Neil sat in the boat (hatless, poor ignorant boy) under a white sun so powerful it seemed to be obliterating matter, after Mike slipped beneath the surface of blue silk.

Mike dove without tanks, used only flippers, face mask, pole-net, plastic bags tucked into the waistband of his trunks. Since Neil couldn't see anything he could only wait, the wooden plank hard under his bony bum, squinting at green-furred mountains, white sky, sapphire water. (What is seldom conveyed by tourist board photos, he told me, is the sense of desolation, of ancient, lush decay.) Sun like burning paste. Neil hunched, gripping his knees, listening to the *plish plish* of seawater licking the hull, almost shivering with worry. Shore was too far to shout to. Even with the spectacles he kept poking up against his nose, he couldn't make anyone out from that distance. If Mike didn't return soon, should Neil try to pilot the boat back, to get help? He'd never touched a boat's motor in his life. He'd never touched a *lawnmower's* motor. And the coral network in the shallows, what if it raked open the hull? Neil didn't like admitting it, but he could not swim. The coral might rake him open. Sharks would come. They could smell blood—he'd read that. And wouldn't help be too late even if he managed to find any? I winced to picture him, sweat beading on his pinking scalp, pink blotches spreading over his long white legs.

He had the "blessed wits," as he puts it, to take off his specs and place them on the bench before leaning his face and then his torso over the boat's side, trying to see anything. It made the backs of his legs tingle having the top half of him cantilevered over the water like that. *Plish, plish* went the ocean against the hull. Young Neil next thought he would try to place his face directly *onto* the water, cool himself a little, maybe open his eyes once there for a better look around. So he kneeled on the boat's rim, believing his feet (braced against the hull) would stabilize him.

And then of course the boat tipped, and over he went.

His torso just got the better of his legs, was all. Neil was certain he would die. Thrashing and spluttering, pumping his legs underwater like a bicyclist, he managed to grab the boat's rim, making the craft list violently, but not so much that it took on significant water. Neil held on, bicycling, panting, praying—that is, he recalls, bargaining: "whatever deals an irreligious man pleads for when he's about to become shark food."

He began chanting in his mind: *get back here get back here get back here. Oh please get back here now. Now. Now, dammit.*

And at last (eternities to Neil) came the geyser-boom of spray, the great gasped inhale, and Mike's shining blond head broke the surface. His face glistened, eyes popped, heaving air (a sound like a jet turbine). One huge, slick brown forearm hooked the boat's side, depositing three knotted plastic bags on the bench at the far end. Then two boulder-sized arms planted themselves, and in a single heave (Neil admiring, despite himself, the upper-body strength it took) Mike flopped himself over the edge, panting and dripping. Without even yanking off his flippers he turned, braced his feet against the boat's sides, took hold of one of Neil's forearms with both his hands and hoisted straight up. Neil banged his shins pretty badly being pulled in; a trickle of blood and painful, purple gashes announced the fact afterward. (He still bears a tiny crescent-shaped scar on each shin, if you look closely amid the coppery down.) But while it happened he could only bless Mike's easy power, hauling him up and in like an awkward, giant catch.

"Thought we'd have ourselves a little cool-off dip?" Mike said.

Then he began to laugh, still breathless from his dive: tremendous shouts of laughter. Neil was spitting water, eyes stinging with salt, shins hurting like hell and bleeding. Speechless with embarrassment, he hung his head—yet could not keep a stupid smile from infiltrating his face, because Mike's merriment held no cruelty. The three bags sat wetly on the boat's floor: clear, squarish balloons, listing a bit. Forgetting his shame and the pain in his shins, Neil groped for his (wet but intact) specs to peer closer. Inside the bags wiggled three small beings of the sort seen on nature documentaries. Mike may as well have rocketed to another galaxy and back with his catch. Two of the creatures, Neil learned later, were a species of angelfish. Velvet black, elegantly striped, two laser-thin lines of electric blue. Their fins trailed elaborate thready tendrils, curling at the tips. The third was a disc of saturated lemon, thin as a coin, flitting and flashing in its water package in the sun—the purity of its yellow a shock. (It struck Neil harder then, than in all his gray youth, how slavishly the eye follows color.) These living beings from another continuum, hopelessly fragile, would sell very well if they survived the air travel. To celebrate (never mind Neil's near-drowning) the young men bought some Hinano beer on their way back, in a Toyota pickup sun-bleached the color of bone, to the frond-roofed shack Mike used. Neil never discovered whose shack it was, nor where the old truck had come from. Rule one, Mike never had money. Meaning, he spent everything he earned. He may have plied his local contacts with beer or fish or goofy charm; maybe part of the deal was that he never stayed long.

Neil describes a sky going teal, then ink, air raucous with bullfrogs—one constant, streaming, multi-part chant replenished in rounds, as if different factions of the chorale were drawing breath. Night on the island came deep, stars many but distant, vaster than any Neil had known. Something pent out there, something he could smell in the blackness—like raw hamburger—made him wildly glad for the hut's flimsy walls, the propane burner, the pan of onions sizzling, the greasy lantern, Mike's gunshot laugh. He watched Mike prepare *poisson cru* on the slab of scarred wood that served as desk, table and cutting board. Mike's hands, oddly demure compared with the rest of him (though reddened by sun and salt), sliced the ahi thin, submerging the slices in a solution of lime juice; soon he would add coconut milk. He paused for pulls of beer, opened his jaws for bites of baguette mashed with wedges of Vache Qui Rit, the cheapest cheese in Papeete groceries.

Mike was a vision then. I still forget this sometimes, but there are photographs. A buck. Body taut, muscled. Hair white-blond, bearded grin, all feckless glamour. Neil, though pink and crisp with sunburn, felt awed, foolishly grateful for the food, the beer, for having escaped the burning blue depths of the sea—for the green, stinky aloe sap on his wounds. Mike had broken a fat spine from the cactus plant and painted Neil's gashed shins with the foul-smelling, snot-like substance that oozed out clear chartreuse. It soothed instantly. All of it as far from the world of suits and ties, filings, depositions as he could dream. Neil's gratitude spread, watching the warm shadows thrown by the lantern, into practical concern for his gentle, Tarzan-like friend.

"How long d'you propose to keep doing this?" Neil asked. He was sitting on a bench in his shorts, burnt legs crossed (green-painted purple dents on each shin), balancing a brown Hinano bottle on one knee. He liked the dry, woven pandanus mat under his bare soles, sliding them back and forth against it.

"Doing what?" Mike's arms moved everywhere, pushing green peppers around, chopping tomatoes, grand smells, crackling sounds, his shadow alert behind him.

"You know. The diving."

"Why would I stop?" Mike looked up, smiling. If you forgot he had scarcely made it out of secondary school, his tone might have suggested the mild intrigue latent in a philosophical point of order. Threads of sun-white hair fell over his browned forehead. Neil watched the knife, tip steady on the wood surface, flash up and down. Small mounds of minced green pepper foamed up on either side.

"I'd imagine it's—er, rough on the health?" Neil stammered. "I mean say, once you've got a bit older?" He didn't want to sound like a *pansy*, a word he'd picked up in freshman months on American soil. Equivalent, he gathered, to *nancy-boy*. But he'd heard about divers' ailments. Depths did strange stuff to a man, stuff that could disable you. And his British education had blasted him from age eleven with the absolutes: You flung yourself through the obstacle course, snatched the degree that fetched a living, pushed pushed pushed else you be left back to rot, to work a trade if any remained. (Shipbuilding was dying then.) Or you'd have to scrape by on the dole. He'd seen plenty of this: filthy hair, skin like old luggage, bad teeth, missing teeth. Including the children.

American largesse, its sheer serenity, baffled him.

Mike blinked, still smiling, gently perplexed. He scratched his bearded cheek, the knife held slack alongside, as though he might commence shaving with it. Instead he used the blunt end to ease the piles of minced pepper into the fragrant stir-fry. The pan's crackling report dulled a moment, then intensified.

"I'll do it till something better shows up."

He grinned again, pleased to've dispatched the small annoyance and revest his attention in what most mattered.

*N*eil spoke of Mike on our first date. Oh, I never forget its anniversary, though he has to be reminded sometimes. Well, men. Quite clear in mind for me, anyway, that windy North Beach afternoon, soft, polleny light. Neil had delivered a box of files to the office where I did transcription. First view: forlorn weedy spectre wavering at my desk, as if just deposited there by aliens. Impossible to miss his Afro, a perfect sphere of red-gold cotton candy. He stared, first at me, then at the little nameplate propped on the desk—RACHEL BLUM—just a printed piece of cardboard in a plastic holder. I had my earphones in, typing away at customary speed. It's an easy living, a bit redundant since I write during off-hours. My shoulders get sore; I make Neil knead them any chance I get. Very fast I am—at transcription I mean. "You don't type, you *surge*," a secretary once told me. I remember Neil made a show of checking his watch that day; then, facing me as if I were a point-blank gun barrel, shouted his invitation to lunch. The whole staff turned to stare. He must've thought I couldn't hear with my earphones in. Poor fellow blushed so hard I thought his head might pop off. I agreed to lunch, partly because of his bravery, partly because I was getting hungry and had only brought an apple that day—but also because of something in his face. As if it posed a question you couldn't not try to answer.

I suppose I look his opposite. Short and urgent, Jewish Carmen to his Ichabod Crane. More *zaftig* in those years, big mane of hair. Still, I fancied myself—what—vital. Curves, good carriage, good breasts. Not beautiful. Certain women are called handsome; I've classed myself (with no one's permission) one of those. Like any healthy woman, I liked feeling heads turn when I entered a restaurant, which I seem to remember they did at the crowded Little City—a noisy *boîte* off Washington Square, now gone many years. Soon we were facing each other in a booth over flutes of icy sauvignon, feeling clever and bold. And somewhere along that airy continuum, Neil began describing his friend Mike Spender. I asked—yelled, you had to yell in Little City during lunch hour—whether Mike had a girlfriend.

"That's a bit tricky," Neil shouted.

He began concentrating on pinching stray crumbs into a line on the tablecloth, soldiers forming flanks.

"Mike's married now. But—it's complicated—he's been known to, ehm, known to—get around."

My expression must have grown grave. Neil glanced up, his red Afro cocked back like a dandelion. His irises are what astonish you: mahogany-brown edges giving over, about a third of the way in, to reddish-caramel centers that somehow exactly, and I mean exactly, matched the caramel highlights in his hair. You forget what is being said, you are so busy falling into those eyes, trying to understand how that *works*, the irises matching the hair. Strangers have since volunteered to me the same blank wonder, when they recall first meeting him.

"Oh, but I'm a couples man m'self!"

He practically fell across the table adding this.

Neil's brogue makes words come out squiggly or stretched. He says *prrrops* for perhaps, *situehtion* and *deffacahlt*. A nasal music. He looked down again, pink at the cheekbones, adjusting plates and silver with furious attention, as if tidying a chessboard.

"Definitely a couples man," he said, nodding at the plates. *Cooples mahn.*

I grew up without siblings in Phoenix, Arizona—little more in those days than a fistful of hopefully named streets in the middle of Martian desert: Willow Thicket Way and Shady Glade Drive. Telephones shared party lines and prefix exchanges; ours, touchingly, was Windsor. My father worked as a mechanic for

TWA at Sky Harbor Airport—its steel tube control tower a bragging point, one of the world's largest then. His face was sunburnt and creased like beef jerky, his nature mild. I remember him in his grimed canvas jumpsuit—there was no knowing its original color—watching the Huntley-Brinkley Report from his (also colorless, also stained) easy chair, holding a glass of Pabst Blue Ribbon. His fingernails and interstitial joints were imbedded with black and he smelled, always, of machine oil and beer. My mother wore a pinafore apron to fix cheeseburgers and tuna salad with red onions, and sat on the toilet with her eyes closed, cigarette in hand, for hours. What saved me was the Phoenix library—a big flat pink building like a sheet cake, air-conditioned. Both parents smiled at the piles of books I hauled home. Both are long dead. I aced my typing class in high school, left Arizona the first year of college and traveled—deciduous trees were a revelation—typing for a living wherever I went, which led to the transcribing in San Francisco.

I'd had men of different sizes, shapes, ages, natures. None stuck. Looking back, I'm pretty sure I assumed (in some mute, buried center of myself) it was because I wasn't beautiful enough. And that this was somehow a moral failing, if not a willed one.

I had also by then lived alone a long while, reached an age where you don't suppose things can change—and where you're crossing, like an international dateline, the limits of that fact's ability to hold anyone's interest. I was writing stories about all this at the time—how else to make sense of it?—evenings, weekends, lunch hours; stories strung like misshapen beads along strings of illicit time. Gazing across the tablecloth at that doleful face under its halo of red, amid the expensive colognes and pan-fried calamari and predator-roar of Little City, I silently composed my first book's dedication.

For the ginger-haired couples man.

$\mathcal{A}$fter he passed the bar, Neil took out a small business loan and opened a personal injury practice, a newish complex across town. His relationship to his work has always made me think of Somerset Maugham's young doctor in *Of Human Bondage*: clientele mostly illiterate vineyard workers, often unwell, ill-washed, confused, sometimes scared. Neil cares for them, gives them close attention, but never lets their stories undo him. Many have been fired—illegally, of course—when they get hurt on the job. Word of mouth (in Spanish, naturally) leads them to Neil, as if to Lourdes. Because "Abercrombie" is too tricky, they call him Señor Neil. They bring him offerings of thanks: tamales, fresh eggs (tan shells, flecks of chicken-poop still stuck to some of them), hand-stitched kerchiefs, carved wood figurines—birds, whistles, vague animal forms, crucifixes. He gives some of the trinkets to his secretaries every year; others he arranges on a shelf in our living room. He never learned Spanish except for a few fundamentals, but this hasn't slowed him; at one point he had three translators working for him. Enough workers got injured, and enough wineries paid up, that he could eventually acquire a mortgage on a 1930s bungalow with a front porch—prices still sane then, before all Mira Flores became boutique real estate. You could walk or bicycle the few blocks from the shady old neighborhood (later ruled Historic District) to the town's Courthouse Square. Through it ran Main, where Mike had Finny Business. Neil rode his bicycle to court and errands (a lengthy apparition pedaling along in a suit; tie flapping off to the side). Often he'd spot Mike in his gunslinger mode, framed in the shop's doorway, smoking, squinting. They would wave at each other, Mike flashing the famous grin. Neil took to stopping in at the aquarium store during lunch hours. And soon Mike began to materialize on Neil's front porch like a conjured genie, clutching two fat cigars—Neil has an unfortunate weakness for these, which I've never been able to rout. The men would settle into plastic Adirondack chairs, feet up on the porch ledge, leaning their heads back now and then to send up puffs of smoke, watching the street, nodding at mothers pushing strollers, bicyclists, dog-walkers.

Neil spent most of those years establishing his practice, but every time he recalls them—to me, because I demand it—he always cites three milestones: Mike hired his assistant full time, went bald, and got married.

"Sweetheart, where's my spice rub?"

"Behind the bread crumbs, where you always keep it."

"Ah, yeah. Can you fetch me a can of anchovies from the lower cupboard?"

"Neilly, do we have to use those?"

I know what I'm risking by objecting. But they're fish-stinky and salty. To me they wreck things.

As I fear, his glance is tight.

"Yes," he says. "We do."

The look, the words: *I know my business, of which you've no grain of comprehension; no course but to rely on my larger knowledge. All will be made clear once you've tasted the product, so kindly stand away and shut up.* But in the case of anchovies, I long to argue, he's just wrong, wrong. You either like fish-stinking salt or you don't: it's not a matter for persuasion. But I'll never win this one, and if I try, especially while he's in the fervor of dinner-prep, the damage, like an oil spill, will be ugly, and take ages to repair. He's often right about many things, which earns him the occasional pigheadedness. And if it weren't for him, as we both know, I'd live on raisin bran and canned soup. Sighing, I reach for the flat, elliptical tin.

"So go on, please."

Arms ablur; eyes resuming their ricochet, cutting board to range top. The dance of the chefs. "Right. Where was I, then?"

"How they met."

∞

NEIL DOESN'T think he ever asked Mike outright. I guess we've always assumed Mike Spender met Tilda Krall at the Porthole, a rat-nest of a bar just three blocks north of Finny Business. The Porthole's neighborhood must have been owned by a distant or indifferent landlord, because the grimy buildings never changed. No windows, no sign. Just the circular hole cut in the pitted brown door: a sightless eye. Bars across it. That door seemed a warning, obdurate and grim as any jail. Leather-clad bikers banged through—Mike talked with them for hours, his Black Beast nosed in among their Harleys like so many gleaming horses out front. Other types lingered at the Porthole, types we've all seen: men and women who feel compelled on a spring day—and spring is shameless here; warm, clear, blossom-scented, carpets of yellow mustard floating across vineyards and fields; avenues of trees flocked pink and white, bits of froth flittering down so the air seems to twinkle, thumb-sized finches pouring out one long silvery trill as if they could not bear to break the note—on that sort of day the types I speak of choose to disappear into a smelly cave and nurse a gin. Much as I love ale myself (but cold, please), I never once considered pushing open the door of the Porthole. God knew what you'd touch if you did. Neil poked his head in a couple of times.

"It's what you'd imagine," was all he'd say.

We know that Tilda had briefly worked in the Legal Aid office after Neil left, but she could have been a biker to look at her. She has a face—it doesn't make me happy to say this—like the faces of the homeless. Leathery, ruddy, gimlet-eyed. I've since seen an old photograph from 1979, when Tilda and Mike were just starting: he was twenty-nine, she nineteen. A black and white. They are seated before someone's desk, as if they were applying for a loan when the camera caught them. Mike, of course, is a smirking satyr, ready for mischief and excess. Tilda looks wary, hair the same lank brown, still cut like a friar's, as if the scissors had traced the rim of a shallow bowl placed back on her head. You could not call her beautiful, but her face had the smoothness of youth, her features pert. A kind of cute tomboy, except for the affectless gaze—unblinking. In the photo she seems to be measuring the photographer for a quick punch in the nose. That expression must have stopped short any pert assumptions, even back then.

Mike would surely, at the beginning, have taken her straightaway on a tour of his shop. And though of course I didn't know them then, I can easily imagine Tilda walking the aisles of tanks, each show starring its different wonder. I can imagine her breathing the pleasantly rank odors, scanning the musty boxes, the aging magazines, books (*Reef Life, Understanding Bettas, A Practical Guide to Corals*). Mike had mounted an old-fashioned diver's suit just inside the entrance to the store. He'd found the thing in Monterey, something out of Jules Verne: scratched and blackened metal armor, empty and stiff, one handless sleeve raised in greeting, the helmet's cross-hatch over the (still-frightening) dark hole where a face would be. I try to think how Tilda's own face must have absorbed this setting, and I cannot envision it once breaking its cool repose. To put it crudely, I don't think the fish and all Mike's prideful knowledge meant a speck to Tilda. I think she wanted sex with Mike Spender, wanted it at once, and made that plain. Neil shrugs whenever I suggest this, which means he can't argue the point. Mike must have been stunned by his luck. Soon the two were seen roaring around town on the Beast, faces squinting and sunburned; soon she moved into his room above the delicatessen downtown—one of those stained old residential hotels. Neither Neil nor I like thinking about the way they probably lived then, between the flophouse room, the deli below (its handy liquor section) and the Porthole. On the other hand they harmed no one, and never pretended to be other than what they were. Isn't there still something to be said for that?

In no time at all, a baby was conceived.

They married in jeans, aloha shirts and flip-flops, at the county administration office. Neil had been recruited as their witness. A set of bobble-headed plastic wedding dolls, white-tulle bride and tux-sheathed groom with timid smiles and Betty Boop eyes, flanked the registration forms on the front counter. The clerks made Mike and Tilda sign a paper confirming they had declined a little handbook which offered to prepare newlyweds for the prospect of sexual congress. Bride and groom had drunk a bottle of cheap champagne for breakfast, and smelled of it. Tilda pinched a winter daisy from the bushes outside the building as they walked in, tucked it behind her ear. Neil waited, slightly back of them, to sign the logbook. It was an unseasonably mild February day, sky a scrubbed blue, backlit puffs of cloud. The group stood outside under a wood trellis entwined with copa de oro vines, though it was still too early for those blooms. Leaves shone. Crows glided, shouting, from tree to tree. Janna, the lady minister, read the vows, looking up by turns from her script to catch their eyes—as if hoping to make some of the language seep in. After signing the papers they all went to eat pork chile verde at a taqueria opposite the hospital (its food, I have to concede, is still terrific). For a honeymoon Mike and Tilda rode the Beast out to Bodega Bay and camped. They built a fire, grilled steaks, flung themselves into the icy surf naked, quaffed Stoli martinis with little onion-stuffed olives from plastic jugs Tilda packed.

At the civil ceremony Tilda kissed Neil on the lips after she kissed Mike. She did not, he has sworn to me, use her tongue. Her breath wafted the sour-bread smell of champagne.

"Thanks, sweetie," she mumbled. *Sweetie* was what she would always call him. Neil could never quite tell, at first, how she meant it. Tilda had a voice to match her face, low and rough. It struck Neil that day (confusing him further) that she was shy—her gruff display part sheltering screen, part bravado. That day, she was smiling. But Tilda's smile would always—as long as we were to know her—be broken, distant, holding to itself some gritty knowledge, something we could not then guess at, however much we tried. There was mockery in it. There was hatred in it. These were not observations you could prove, or defend.

Tilda grew a belly. It required, Neil noted, no costume change. She already preferred men's shirts, jeans, moccasins. Because the pending baby made their flophouse room infeasible, Mike borrowed money from his mother, Louise. (His ma lamented his western life, Mike told Neil; she wished he'd move back in with her. Refused to visit, but could not begrudge her only son these bits of funding.) He paid first and last month's rent on a dessicated barn, a west county acre near the apple orchards, and with the old Portuguese landlord's permission (or so Mike told it) he set about to "renovate." Rent was cheap then—everything was; how it grieves us now—the area colder, closer to the ocean, hilly with apple orchards, storybook pretty. Mike traded his Beast for a rusting Volkswagen bus. Then he cashed in some of the bonhomie he'd invested during those years of downtown vigil, marshaling friends and their vehicles. They helped him haul a bunch of scrap milled lumber, left in piles from the demolished old county airport, to his acre.

"Yo *Bernie!*" His hale, like his laugh, so loud it stopped passersby, made them look around sharply for its source. He'd stride from his doorway, Neil recalls, his grin a bank of headlights, throw a ham-thick arm over the shoulders of the bar buddy or the guy who ran the newsstand or the pasty counter clerk who fixed his hoagie at lunch. He'd walk with his mark, talking like a statesman—and in minutes had his promise of manpower and wheels.

It made Mike uneasy to be away from his fish for long, but he drove into town to check on them every few days. The kid who worked as his assistant (a patient, sweet-faced boy named Ben) managed it so nothing died during Mike's absences. Mike was fiercely proud of his stock's low mortality and disease rates—results, Mike declared more than once, of pristine conditions, correct chemical balances, careful pairing, and so forth. Sometimes a new batch of fry would have arrived to greet Mike on his visits back. This event—a gelatinous cloud of sparks, twitching—made him radiant as if he'd spawned the fry himself. Which in a midwife kind of way, he had. Though there's never a guarantee they'll survive, the appearance of fry is always an excellent sign. Mike would rush to the tank in which the births had occurred, squat before the glass, eyes blazing.

"Will you look at that," he'd breathe.

He also set about taking down the barn and, saving what he could of that lumber, built a house on his grassy plot. The idea was to finish by late fall, with the end of Indian summer and dry weather—also when the baby happened to be due. His friends helped, many of them terrifying looking bikers from the Porthole: two plumbed and wired for him. From early morning you'd see them out there, Mike surveying progress from the land's gentle rise alongside, standing like an overfed Superman: legs apart, fists on hips, red-and-yellow aloha shirt flapping in the wind. Neil showed up to help on weekends, though he warned them of his "two left hands." Mike's friends looked on Neil with amusement. Usually, he told me, they'd only let him hold a board steady while one of them ran the saw. (Sometimes he'd shoot one hand up to push tight his spectacles. Thinking about this alarms me even in retrospect.) Weekdays were filled with hammer whacks, whining saws, drills, power tools—someone had lugged over a generator; long rubber cords crisscrossed the grass. Before the kitchen functioned Tilda set up a hibachi grill in the back, gave everyone beer, slices of American cheese with stolen apples, teriyaki chicken, potato chips. As evenings came earlier and temperatures dropped they built a fire in the yard, passed around gallon bottles of Carlo Rossi. Someone always produced a spliff or two, the unsifted shake and seeds that clawed your throat, made you choke and drool. (Tilda refrained from smoking weed while pregnant, but took small amounts of beer or wine. "Good for them both," Mike growled.) The house emerged as a hexagon—whether intentionally or not, no one knew. It looked like a B-movie spaceship hoving into view as you drove up. People parked chock-a-block on the grass right in front. Mike rigged an outdoor shower around back, shielded from view on two sides. Eventually they got hot water through it. And within a high chicken-wire enclosure (because of deer), Tilda started a garden, with herbs.

"Oh, those were some times," Neil says. He pauses in the chopping to push his specs up.

The structure wasn't finished when the infant girl came, just before Thanksgiving, 1980; possibly it never would be. But it put a roof and walls between the family and the ocean fog, which swept over from the coast at night like a cool quilt. They named the baby Astrid, in honor of the stars. When she was toddling the baby would point at herself and enunciate, as best she could, the name she'd heard them call her: *Add-dee* (just as moon, for a good while, was *nu-nu*). Everyone took it up and she was Addie thereafter: a blonde sprite with her father's dark brows and richly lashed brown eyes, precocious, sturdy, willing at a moment's notice to hop into the rusting van and drive to the Mexican coast for camping, fishing, and startling mishaps she withstood like a soldier—the bloodied toe when the nail ripped off, the vomiting of barbecued oysters, the jellyfish stings. At home Tilda let the child run about in dirty shorts, cadge meals with neighbors, collect rocks, bones, lizards, fallen apples, free as a dog. Mike adored his little daughter, and whenever she appeared his big-nosed, sunburned face broke into creases. (He'd lost his hair by this time, head a huge red egg.) When she was new he'd stalk the property with the infant stowed under his arm head-forward like a sack of feed—talking to her, "flying her" over the trickle of a creek, her firm belly taut in the palm of his hand, pointing out the wild turkeys that pecked at the edge of the property, the doe and fawn stepping delicately, ears flicking. Once she could walk, the two squatted in Tilda's garden under fierce sun, picking cucumbers, tomatoes, butter squash, mint. (Addie loved ladybugs, loved to watch the bright shells scuttle over her arm, sprout polka-dot wings, zoom off.) Her father performed for her, singing, mugging. Addie begged for the Nickel Trick, executed out in the yard while Tilda grilled burgers or chicken legs. Mike would set aside his beer, rest three nickels across the backs of his knuckles, jerk his fist upward so the coins flew into the air, and with the same hand snatch each in rapid succession as it fell, grab-grab-grab before the coins hit the ground. Addie would clap her hands, scrinch up her baby shoulders as if delight might overflow out her ears, laughing.

"Do 'gain, Daddy."

When she was older Mike brought her to the store on weekends. He gave her tasks: polishing the tank glass fronts with Windex and paper towels, washing the abalone shells he kept in a basket, until their opal linings glistened. To please Addie he acquired a pair of seahorses; they nodded along graceful and calm beneath the surface, translucent when light caught them. She loved them, loved all the stock down to the lowliest snails, the whiskered bottom-feeders; she memorized their names. At five she could advise customers on matters of food, tank-cleaning, plants, breeding. Neil observed this on his lunch hours, keeping his face solemn as he shook her hand in greeting. She knew which fish were jumpers, prone to flinging themselves from the water at the first opportunity.

"Keep your lids closed!" she'd call after buyers as they exited, with the weary stoicism of one who'd seen the worst.

*A*fter Addie began grade school, Tilda found afternoon work in one of the first franchise bookstores to sprout in Mira Flores (just a corridor of shops at the time, perpendicular to the street). No one viewed the Book Stash as a threat then—everyone still too drugged by the fresh sharp smell of pines in warm sun, the drifty morning fog, heavy sweetness of roses spilling over fences in Popsicle colors, faint salt scents of ocean, of burnt toast and weak coffee from Adele's, the twenty-four-hour diner. (You can still look into Adele's big front window from the street at any hour and view a passable enactment of Edward Hopper's *Nighthawks*.) Not even the owners of the Masthead seemed worried; at least, that's how Neil tells it. Their used-books shop a block away, pungent with mildew and pipe tobacco, had been around as long as anyone could remember. The stores coexisted without fuss for a number of years. It's hard to explain those times—though Neil tries quite often—before the dozen other malls, before the viral McMansions blanketing surrounding hills, the big-box super-stores selling cargo-containers of goods to 300-pound citizens. Before the freeway became a frenzied, roaring, twenty-four-hour rapids you entered at mortal peril.

As best as anyone could tell, Neil says, Tilda liked her work. It took her out of the country for a while each day. Mike had found her a used blue Datsun which Addie immediately named Dottie; Tilda drove it to work after dropping Addie at school. She liked looking at cookbooks, co-workers remember. The Book Stash dwelt near enough to Finny Business that she and Mike could lunch together before Tilda started her shift. Her co-workers assumed, Neil later learned, that those lunches involved a lot of liquid of the high-octane sort, because they could smell it on her when Tilda arrived. The Book Stash owners, an aging, fusty couple, visited twice a year from the charter store in Anchorage, Alaska. They inspected all job applications, with other documents mailed weekly to them (before ubiquitous fax machines). The owners were aware that Tilda had a child. So when their store manager, a tensile brunette with a ponytail, complained by long distance that Tilda smelled boozy after lunch—though her performance never seemed impaired—the owners suggested gentle tactics at first, like leaving spearmint gum and mints near the timecards.

Cass Medford, the slender, tart young manager—Neil wound up meeting her at the police station—would stand afternoons in the bookstore's windowless back room with her exacto-blade, slicing open carton after carton of foil-embossed paperbacks, oblivious to the breasty wenches on the covers, swooning in the arms of muscular rogues. As she worked, Cass confessed to Neil, she'd tried to make sense of her unease. Something about the new employee chafed at her, something she couldn't name, creepier and more troubling than the vodka breath. It vexed her that she couldn't identify, let alone dispel, the intangible thing. Tilda was not a surly worker. She straightened shelves, boxed returns, located titles without complaint, joked with staff and customers. But something glinted (and that was the only word Cass could find) behind Tilda's words and motions. Cass tried to offer what she considered upbeat attention to the new woman. (This took form as a slap on the back. Speaking with Cass, Neil notes, was a bit like chewing raw ginger.) "Hey there!" she'd bark, tilting her head back, squinting through thick lenses—milk-glass under fluorescent tube-light. That was the sum of her greeting to employees arriving for their shifts; her farewell as she herself hurried out the door.

The employees—most very young—didn't, they told Neil, worry about Cass. They liked Tilda, though she was older than themselves. They lived in complicated states of transit as befits the young; their attentions dreamy, their requirements cheerfully few.

Which was why what happened, confounded them.

❦

REMEMBER, NEIL always cautions me, that Mike never earned much at Finny Business. He plowed back any profit into buying new stock for the store, always in pairs, to try to breed them. Though Tilda later made clear to Neil what she thought of this habit ("like selling the family cow for a handful of beans"), she had long since chosen to ignore it, perhaps wisely, as a fixture of character. Tilda's own pay, of course, was minimal. Though their rent was modest, and the old Portuguese landlord so consistently absent they sometimes wondered whether he'd died, the Spenders' handling of money could best, Neil says, be described as childlike—the boozy lunches an example. Basic costs had pinned them against that awful wall, where they lay awake at night wondering what they could sell. Tilda and Mike had nothing to sell. The van limped; Dottie Datsun couldn't go faster than forty. Addie wore secondhand things; the whole family did. But in those days nobody cared, and Tilda had always been good at ferreting deals from consignment racks. Strangely, Neil says, she and Mike seldom fought about money. Perhaps Tilda never brought it up. Mike remained oblivious as ever, though he sometimes made noises at dinner about grand plans. He would whisk them all down to Tahiti one day, he promised his wife and child. Bora Bora. They would drink coconut milk through a straw from a hole in the shell, walk on roads of crushed white coral, flakelike stones warm and smooth against bare feet; for breakfast they would spoon up the rosy sweet flesh of papayas big as your head. Bananas the size of your arm, purple and orange. These particulars, Mike told Neil, always made Addie's eyes kindle.

Tilda's eyes, we've assumed, never flickered.

❦

THAT WAS also an era when Mike regularly strode unannounced into Neil's office after work (brushing the objecting secretaries aside like so many cobwebs), insisting Neil come home with him that night to have supper with the family. Neil ate alone often enough then that he welcomed the company. He also felt it would have been unkind to refuse, though he could see the level of the Spenders' struggle once he'd entered the spaceship house: pots of leftover soup, dried rinds of it crusting the rim, plastic bags of discount outlet bread, the sort that wads into balls to feed ducks at the park, often a green rash of early mold stippling the far end of the loaf. Unmade beds, rugs spackled with caked mud. Perhaps the cleanest household element was the simple aquarium Mike had rigged in the living room. The fish were basic, a few swordtails, guppies—royal blue, with yellow fantails—a handful of mollies, zebra danios, tetras. He'd installed a taffy-like knot of driftwood in the gravel; the fish loved its crannies for hiding, mating, staking territory. His plants shone, lace and bamboo, a jungle of green filigree. The tank's lights were soft: a big box of blue sending up streams of silver spheres night and day, making that soothing laboratory noise, the fish lively and alert in their sparkling world. The Spenders' cat, Bud—an ugly tabby Addie insisted they adopt when it wandered in from nowhere, named by Mike for the beer in his hand the night the animal arrived— sat for hours watching the burbling tank and its occupants as if trying to solve a colossal riddle, the tip of its tail ticking.

Mike and Tilda hadn't set out to run what people called a crash pad. But someone could most always be found bunking on their couch—the mini-bottle of Suave shampoo in the tub corner, the discolored razor near the sink—guests whose stories were vague and complex, who owned less, if possible, than the Spenders did; tightlipped men and women who stumbled off to undocumented futures. Yet for all its mess, Neil said, the Spender place gave off a galloping vitality: plates strewn, books and bed-clothes piled, half-consumed cups of cocoa and coffee and bowls of cereal, opened newspapers sifted about as if abandoned at some Pompeiian moment; crayons, chipped game board tokens, thousand-piece puzzles fractionally assembled, nubby stuffed animals leaking little turds of cotton batting. A glass jar (packed with more roots than water) held a sweet potato; from its crown a bundle of green vines, arm-thick, poured to the floor. And for a centerpiece the bubbling tank, whose occupants darted like arrows of light.

Neil poked his head, that first visit, into the rooms down the hall. Mike and Tilda's bedroom looked as though a burglar had ripped it apart. Clothing dropped, bedding twisted, papers snowing from every surface, empty glasses, mismatched shoes. The sight shocked Neil ("I could never live that way," he's admitted to me)—though his eyes also registered the books stacked by each side of the mangled bed, the pages' outside edges stenciled with the county library's imprint. He resolved at once to research how much the family owed in back fines, and clear the debt.

He moved on quickly.

Addie's room, by contrast, testified to the girl's vision: bed neatly made, pink chenille ridges rippling concentrically. Along its head a half-dozen small pillows, arrayed so each edge just over-lapped the next. Against these, at dead center, she had propped a wide pink fan painted with cherry blossoms—perhaps Tilda had gleaned it from a secondhand shop. On the girl's bureau sat a clear bowl of colored glass pebbles, three sand dollars, two elastic ponytail ties tangled with fine blonde strands that caught light. A plastic palomino wore a gold heart locket on a chain around its proud neck. Peach cologne in a peach-shaped bottle, the glass stem its stopper. Tacked to the wall, photographs, evenly spaced: the Taj Mahal, a koala bear clinging to a tree trunk, a flamenco dancer in fiery mid-whirl. Neil's eyes drifted from the posters to Addie's window, and through it spied the family clothesline in the backyard.

Every garment he saw pinned to those lengths of line in the pale sun—aloha shirts and work shirts, underpants, t-shirts, jeans, shorts—struck Neil as the most faded, threadbare togs he could remember seeing.

It caught, he told me, at something in his sternum.

He accompanied the family to the drive-in movies. Drive-ins still did good business then. They saw *Batman*, *Indiana Jones*, *Back to the Future*. The first time, when the Spenders pulled off to the road's shoulder to discuss which adult should be bundled through the admissions gate in the car's trunk, Neil insisted on paying for the evening, and for every drive-in outing thereafter. He let the family give him dinners enough so that (in his mind, at least) everyone could keep some dignity.

One autumn night when Neil had been corralled over by Mike, he found Tilda setting an oblong platter of filet mignon on the table, choice pieces. Neil was learning to cook; he recognized the quality of the cuts, and knew their cost. He worried his presence at dinner may have caused his friends to break the bank, and said so.

"Tilda, aren't these terribly expensive? Ye haven't been extravagant on my account, have ye?"

Tilda had placed a dish of fresh radishes and green onions on the table, and was salting them. She wore her usual man's shirt and jeans, barefoot (the cat pressing itself between her ankles, mewling nonstop), a dishtowel over her shoulder. Dutch boy hair curtained an eyebrow. For an answer she turned and lifted her shoulder-strap bag into the air—a huge shapeless tote, woven in Navajo design—as if she were hoisting the hand of a triumphant boxer.

She cocked her head at Neil, shut her eyes (Tilda has the inexplicable habit of shutting her eyes when she speaks). Smiled.

"No worries, sweetie," she said, eyes closed. "Five-finger discount."

She set the bag down, glanced at him and waggled her fingers, a mock-coquette. She had spoken beguilingly, but it was at just such moments, shrouded in those coy tones, Neil said, that he felt the hatred beneath her words, glittering like a pair of eyes. Not hatred of *him*, precisely. But of what then, or whom? She reached to her feet and lifted Bud with two hands under his soft striped belly, placing him outside the open back door. The animal shot back in soon as he landed, back paws kicking high as a rabbit's, racing for the kitchen.

Down the hall Addie and Mike could be heard in the bathroom, washing for dinner. Over the splash of running water came Mike's boom-bear voice: "Row, row, row your boat"; six-year-old Addie's piping tones echoed the melody, trying to come in on the second round: their *merrily merrilys* quickly tangled, then collapsed in a rain of laughter, his low and rich, hers like high bells.

Mike started up again. "Row, row, row your boat—"

Early October. Warmth still fingered the cooling air, cool breath from the earth rising alongside the juicy-char smell of the steaks. The lowering sun threw mango light over the room's walls—over the posters tacked there, among them (as if anticipating that light) Gauguin's *Vahine No Te Vi*. A dozen finches hopped in the willow outside—Mike had planted it at the time they built the house; rapidly it had gained girth and branches and jade-colored leaves. The finches made tiny, peeping sounds through the open back door.

Neil stared at Tilda while he pushed with one foot at the cat, which had begun pressing itself with frantic speed between his own ankles under the table. Tilda returned his gaze evenly. *Practical fact*, said her face. A certain amusement flicked across it, and a satisfaction—within that, a venality—Neil could not miss. The cat pressed in and around, *mmroww*ing nonstop, maddened by the smell of the meat.

Why don't they just shut the bloody back door, was what Neil heard himself wonder.

$\mathscr{P}$olice have a name for a practice in the world of retail theft, when a clerk seems to ring up a sale but secretly collects the cash. A pocket case, they call it. The clerk punches a key that opens the register drawer without recording the charge; at the same time, announces the amount due. The customer will tend to pay more attention to the clerk's voice chiming with the sound of the opening drawer, handing the clerk his money. The clerk makes correct change, bags the item, and after the customer has left, pockets the money. It's a guessing game, because a customer may produce a credit card or write a check. But if that happens, the clerk can simply close the drawer and ring up the item the conventional way, with no one wiser.

Neil told me the police nickname. For all I know it may be impossible to carry off anymore. Computer registers are worlds more sophisticated; employers keep surveillance cameras, "integrity shoppers" cruise retail floors to test employee honesty. But in an earlier era the scam was doable, with relative discretion and ease. And Tilda did it.

At first, a little. Then a lot.

Cass Medford grew alarmed, she told Neil, when inventory numbers began contradicting figures for receivables. Small disparities weren't uncommon, but this series' steady climb caught the Alaska managers' attention: they instructed Cass to investigate at once. She said nothing to any employee but arranged, without delay, to spy. It turned out to be as sorrowfully simple as standing outside the bookstore's front window, just back of the line of vision from within.

It was one of those afternoons the townspeople cherish about autumns here: sky a deep, aching blue, motes of gold in the air— so lovely, Cass allowed to Neil, she had considered taking the day off. Leaves had begun to flush crimson, wine, umber; days filled with a warm-sugar smell. Around and through lazed scents of cola, hot pretzels, smoke from leaf fires (still legal), cut-grass, geraniums. Tips of trees barely stirred. In the hills the vines had given up their precious roe and turned to ridge upon brimming ridge of tarnished gold. Gardens hung heavy with their last great loads, tomatoes, eggplant, green peppers. Light felt spun, the color of whipped honey, hovering over the stillness. The whole town, the county, the whole world seemed briefly suspended inside one of those globe spheres—except instead of crystal, the sphere might be one big fire opal.

A glorious, sad, fire opal time.

In the mall, mothers tugged little kids clutching orange and black promotional balloons from the back-to-school sales. Cass walked the long way round the buildings, through the parking lot, so as not to be seen from the Book Stash display window. Nearing the store, she passed a small boy trudging beside his mother; as they walked she heard the boy declare with firmness:

"I'm ready. I'm ready to be grown."

The bookstore's long front counter stood at a right angle to the display window. By edging up from the rear and flattening herself against the outside wall like a *noir*-movie sleuth, Cass gained a clear, full-body, back view of Mrs. Spender at the register. Cass watched a harried, middle-aged man buy an atlas— probably for a teenager beset by homework, she thought. He paid in cash. She watched Tilda smile and thank the man, send him on his way with his purchase. And then, agog, Cass watched the worn green bills slip into Tilda's pants pocket. Tilda then busied herself straightening items on the counter, and when she must have decided no one was near, stooped and transferred the bills from her pocket into her blobby Navajo tote bag—a bag Cass had always detested—heaped on the floor near her feet.

Heart pounding, Cass made a wide return loop on foot, so as not to cross the display window at close hand. She entered

the store quietly, nodding in what she hoped looked like a typi-
cally offhand acknowledgment to Tilda still presiding at the front
counter, and phoned the police from the back room. When the
two uniformed officers showed up—blueblack uniforms, silver
buckles clinking as they walked, a genital jumble of nightsticks
and guns—Tilda, still manning the front counter, directed them
jovially to the back room: "Hey, Jimmy. Hey, Ralph. How's it
hanging?" Cops cruised the stores all the time—security inspec-
tions, auction tickets, toy drives, boredom. In those days you
came to know everyone in minutes: the mailman with his gold-
rimmed teeth, the acne-pocked checkout kid at Bel Air Market,
the hunchbacked old lady who worked crossing guard duty in
front of the grade school weekday mornings. Tilda knew these
people's names, their kids' and grandkids' names and ages; she
kept track of spousal quarrels, vacation plans, bowling scores,
barbecue sauce secrets (coffee, a little chocolate). But when
Jimmy and Ralph and Cass emerged together from the back,
looking grave under the fluorescent ceiling lights, Cass told Neil,
she never forgot the way Tilda's face changed.

"It got dark. Her face, I mean. Dark as if it would explode.
And her eyes, their color. Kind of yellow-green, like flames. I felt
as if we were closing in on an animal."

Cass Medford considered herself an exceptionally strong
young woman. She lived alone, performed unpleasant chores with
no help. She set traps for rats and disposed of their stiffening
bodies, chopped firewood, changed her car's oil, even dabbled in
basic plumbing. But she recalled that she trembled all over a long
time after the officers arrested Tilda.

Tilda stood still and silent while poor Jimmy and Ralph, miserable with their sworn duty, mumbled her rights. Her eyes never
left those of the horrified Cass. Then Cass watched the officers
accompany Tilda out into the warm, vanilla-smelling afternoon,
to drive her in the squad car to the station. They flanked her,
Cass remembers, but did not touch her. Shortly thereafter, Neil
received his call.

"GOOD CHRIST!"

My heart is thumping, heavy and slow. He'd never told me this part before.

"Neilly, this is too horrible. What about Addie? Where was Addie? Did she ever find out?"

Neil pauses over the bowl of raw baby red potatoes. Sunday afternoon, late October. A time of day, before I met him, that used to make me sick with loneliness. Streets empty. Birds go quiet, air chills fast. A good time for filling the kitchen with oven warmth, heavy scents of lamb, garlic. I've put on Tal Farlow, "Have You Met Miss Jones." I know, after these years, what music he can and cannot stand.

He takes a sip of wine.

"Best I can say, Addie was never allowed to know. Almost no one knew, in fact. I posted Tilda's bail that afternoon—it wasn't that terribly much," he adds, so quietly I have to strain to hear. He is chopping the baby reds into quadrants; sprinkling them with rosemary needles stripped from the bush out front. The rosemary's sharp green scent drapes the air, already rich with lamb.

"Phone calls were made," Neil says as he works.

Told that Tilda was unwell, the mother of a classmate of Addie's agreed to collect both girls from school that day, and keep Addie for an ad hoc overnight.

Mike arrived at the cop station—a big brown arm and hand cupping a cigarette out the driver's window of the van. (He had closed the store early, hanging his BACK SOON, PLEASE COME AGAIN! sign, featuring a smiling purple fish and bubbles, finger-painted by Addie.) Mike emerged from the vehicle expressionless. He thanked Neil tersely, offered to reimburse the bail Neil had fronted—Neil refused, of course, knowing very well that Mike had nothing to reimburse with. Mike drove Tilda to her Datsun, still parked downtown. Then the couple drove home in two cars.

By the time they were driving, Neil said, the sun had gone; air turned frosty. A massive, chalk-white moon had risen, surreal as a paste-on appliqué at the edge of the sky. What man and wife thought about as each drove home in the bright moonlight, or what transpired between them when they got there, Neil would never know, though it chewed at his mind for quite some while. He'd replay that day in his thoughts for months afterward, trying to read something more from it than it seemed able to yield. Concerned as he felt for Mike, confused as he felt, the event was never mentioned between the men again. At the police station Mike had spoken little apart from thanking Neil, and had scarcely looked at Tilda, nor she at him. A grimness dulled Mike's eyes, Neil said, as if a familiar duty were required of him, as if Tilda's penchant for theft were like a secret history of seizures— something they'd always controlled privately, but never expected to happen in public.

After Mike and Tilda left the station, Cass Medford drove up—assured in advance by phone that Tilda would be gone—to give a statement, and talk at length with Neil. After sending her home Neil walked straight to the offices of the local paper of record, the *Courier*, for a chat with the man who typed up the weekly police blotter. He wouldn't elaborate to me how he did it, but he succeeded: the incident did not make print. In a community of that size, in that period—I could appreciate what that meant. Neil also prevailed when Tilda's hearing came up, persuading the young, prematurely white-haired Judge Ross McNair (whom Neil knew to be humane, and perhaps a hair partial to Scottish ancestry) to handle the matter discreetly; Neil offered personal recognizance in the case. Tilda was eventually given a stern reprisal in the Judge's private chambers, and sentenced to a number of hours of community service. She wound up fulfilling most of these by collecting excess fruit, orchard-drops, for the town's food bank.

Tilda thanked Neil exactly once at the police station, *sotto voce*. When she did, it seemed to Neil she barely met his eyes. Her face, he told me, showed no remorse, no anger or sadness, no emotion. He couldn't explain it. Her face, he finally said, was absent: as if its owner had simply gone somewhere more interesting.

*A*ddie turned eight that year, 1988.

In years to follow she grew in beauty, a fact that gave wonder to everyone—not least to Mike and Tilda, always drolly aware they weren't exactly the world's most handsome parents. In a photo Tilda showed me long after Addie had herself become a mother, Addie the child stands placidly before the camera in the middle of an empty dirt road. Feet apart, arms held behind her by the elbows like a statesman, wearing a costume of her own careful devising: naked but for a homemade headband and loincloth, a benign redux of *Lord of the Flies*. In the photo she has covered herself scalp to toe in wet black mud which has dried to a crust; her cheeks and forehead are striped with bright blue paint. The photo told worlds: how free the child had been to invent and reinvent herself, the whole of her girlhood. Her character flowed, Neil remembers, as sweetly as it had in the days of ladybugs and the Nickel Trick; her laughter as clear and melodic, her brow as untroubled. One of life's little jack-in-the-box punch lines: some children just grow up good. Addie did not scheme or lie, nor did her brown eyes simmer with the poisoned light that signals the onslaught of puberty. Instead her eyes remained steady and calm, with a patience so refined it struck many as a form of stubbornness. She still helped Mike weekends at Finny Business—she knew enough by then to handle the place alone. But she could only spare the store an hour or two, because she had to attend band practice (jazz trombone), track (relay), and the myriad, complex back-and-forths with girlfriends and boy-friends that required Mike or Tilda (and sometimes Uncle Neil) to drive and drive and drive. She joined Girl Scouts, then 4-H. She raised rabbits. She camped and hiked; sang in glee club, ran for student body treasurer (A VOTE FOR ADDIE IS A $MART VOTE, scotch-taped to halls and message boards). She spent weeks con-cocting a sticky paste-and-clay model of Japan, rising from its painted-board turquoise sea on the dining table. She excelled in math and science, determined even then to be a civil engineer. Somehow, Addie was coming of age in a shockingly normal way. Mike became almost shy around his daughter, but Tilda took it matter of factly. Addie's beauty and offhand goodness seemed, at least to hear Tilda tell it, one more thing to brag about, like a perfectly realized dish.

Neil became convinced, during those years, that Addie existed as a sort of corrective thrown in by nature—one of those goofily sublime afterthoughts—to balance, or even render comic, what-ever it was Tilda and Mike were amounting to.

"*S*hall we use the Avignon tablecloth?"

Neil looks up from rinsing his cutting board, a tired smile. "Why not."

We'd bought it together one windblown morning, in delicate sunlight, from an outdoor vending cart—the bright Provençale samples, red, yellow, green, flapping and snapping in the gusts. *Trop de vent*, the saleswoman had complained, unmoved by my emotional praise of the place. It was no question windy as hell, our hair flying at lunatic angles or, comically, straight up. But good: a good time for us, Avignon. We wandered castles, trying to absorb their convoluted history; ate at a restaurant called Forchette, much too expensive and heart-hostile; searched the tables for Sir Alec Guiness, who was said to favor the place. Stood at the famous bridge while I sang to Neil its wistful, eerie song, *l'on y danse tous en rond*. He bought me a slim gold band at a jeweler's along the main street. We'd just wandered in, and I looked and admired, and he said, so let's then. I still recall the fawning saleswomen, cold sleek mannequins, faces pinched with obvious pain into crooked phony smiles murmuring *C'est vous, madame*. And I feared, for a long time, to wear the ring, feared it might hex our happiness somehow. But by the time I gathered nerve to slip it on we'd been married for years, and I thought nothing could scare me anymore.

I bend to open the bottom drawer, fishing for the folds of green and yellow, the black olive branches strewn across. The cloth has gone a bit shiny with age. Like us?

"Sweetheart, go on. The women."

It was the part of Mike's history Neil had tried to describe during that first North Beach lunch; I'd pulled back at the time, as if from a burn. But now I want to hear it, because information is better (so I reason) than its lack.

He sighs, toweling off.

As far back as Tahiti the women went, he says. To the toothless, bra-wearing, trunk-thick *mamans* hanging clothes outside the frond huts, shining babies all colors of roasted nuts playing in the dirt. Or the young women in the Papeete bars, also missing teeth, who if given enough bad wine or Hinano bounced in your lap, ham-solid rumps wrapped in flower-print *pareu*, singing (nasal voices that also chanted strange, many-part harmonies for Sundays or feast days, sitting cross-legged in tight, concentric rows of circles, leaning back and forth to make a human bellows): *ce soir, nous allons danser . . . sans chemise, et sans pantalon*, and another less coherent one about trying to find a *robinet*; and one or another of the delirious crew from Papeete harbor, sunburnt to near-black, would attempt an impromptu striptease in the warm night until he lost balance and pitched from the sticky tabletop to the floor in a blackout, still grinning though his eyes had rolled up like a pair of summer awnings. It went further back than even that, but only if you started counting early.

All this from Mike's lips to Neil's ears, as it were.

"Some were, unfortunately, from the Porthole." Neil flicks the starchy material over the table, smoothes fabric at his end.

"Ugh." I smooth it at mine.

Past tense, I tell myself. Past tense is a fixity. No return on dredging there.

Some of the women were lonely shopkeepers Mike had been schmoozing since Finny Business opened. Neil got trapped sometimes, meeting this or that one when he'd stroll with Mike on downtown rounds. It embarrassed Neil to the roots of his mercurochrome hair. Those *rencontres* occurred well after Mike was installed in the spaceship house with Tilda; Addie then a blonde elf. The two men walked smack into one of them, a winter after-noon. (Our winters can snap down tight: a single, close sheet of gray, with very fine cold rain, drops so small they're more a steadily falling sheen.)

"Impossible to miss her," Neil says. She stood on the sidewalk arranging sale racks of knit skirts, sweaters, her dyed-dark hair crimped from winter moisture and a trendy perm; she resembled the French writer Collette. Heavy set, too much makeup—

Neil shrugs, positioning a tall ceramic pitcher at the table's center. He's filled it with stems of dried lavender, which he grows out back.

"There was something about her."

"Men read certain signals," he adds, sighing again. "She was fat, really."

He has moved back to the wooden island, commenced driz-zling the chopped potato pieces and rosemary with olive oil, salt, pepper, tosses them in a bowl.

I fold my arms, waiting.

"Face painted up. Tarty. Could have fallen out the door of a pub. Ponged to heaven of some horrible perfume. Wore one of those toga-type ensembles you see on older ladies. No idea how old she was. Forty, fifty? I hadn't been looking in front of me while I rambled along beside Mike. I'd been watching his face, as usual—so bright and animated, nattering on about his new stock. *Sea squirts*, for Lord's sake. For the simulated tide pool. Ever seen sea squirts, Rae? Like coils of wet dung. And *eels*, would you believe. Happy as Christmas, over a pair of eels. Do you know that eels' teeth point *backward*, so that if they get a good grip on your flesh—"

"Stop it, Neilly!" I press my palms over my ears. "I don't want to know that part."

"But why anybody in their proper mind—well, right. Anyway, that's what I was thinking. When I blundered—we blundered—straight into her."

Mike had burst into cascades of affection.

"*Mamie*, my darling! My little kissing gourami!"

Quick as lightning Mike slipped behind the big woman, clamped his huge arms around her, grasping each of her breasts like two great loaves—whisked her from her sales racks, clothes swinging on their hangers as her hands let go.

"Och," Neil clucks, washing his hands of olive oil.

"He reminded me of one of those male pigeons trying to mount a hen. Cooing and burring, snugged in from behind, dancing about, babbling the daftest nonsense. Singing the show-tune 'Mame'—must've been an old joke between them—waltzing her about. Arms round her, pawing, crooning. Like one of those vaudeville sorts."

Neil shakes his head, scatters the salted, oiled potatoes onto a flat pan. I suppress the urge to snatch one up and bite it like an apple.

"Go on."

What bothered Neil was how visibly the woman called Mamie seemed to enjoy it. Like a dry plant getting water, she brightened and colored (makeup or no) beneath Mike's attentions, nesting her cheek alongside his as though that were the most natural place in the world for it—as though they'd rehearsed this little impromptu choreography—more, though, Neil said, as though these lavishments were not only something due her but long *over*due. She didn't seem to notice Neil standing there, staring. Mike must have overtaken all her vision, like a total eclipse.

Suddenly she stopped Mike's dancing. Turned in his arms to face him, looked up at him, searching. As if she were remembering some urgent, consuming question.

For an answer, Mike only beamed down at her with absolute tenderness.

Neil slides the pan into the hot oven alongside the meat, taking care not to let the door bang shut. He is frowning.

"I mean, you'd have thought they were fiancés," he says. "I was gobsmacked. Except what made it different from that, from fiancés, was, ah, her—her—"

"Neediness?"

I do my best to sound mellow and scholastic, leaning against the sink with my arms folded, as though all that can matter is retrieval of the accurate word. But I feel my heart tolling, slow and hard, under my arms. I am thinking, *Why must this be the story, over and over and over*. Dear God the durability, the *resilience* of this bitterly dreary script. Scratch any history, up it pops. Send it off in a space capsule, rubber-banded to a message like a ransom note: *Yes, here's what we mainly got up to during our little tenure. We contained polio and smallpox, built dams and ballparks and diving bells, split the atom, cloned genes. We also liked to kill and torment each other, liked that very much. But here is the ultimate grail among the spoils, what we desired first and last.*

What emblem for it, though? What image?

"Are you listening, Rae?" Neil asks. He's piling pans beside the sink; they bang and clang landing atop each other. "Because really I would just as soon not—"

"I'm listening," I say evenly. It would do well to look busy.

"Please continue," I say, opening the refrigerator. "Shall I make a salad?"

"That was the day it dawned on me."

Neil dries his hands for the dozenth time.

He moves to the cupboards—30s relics, pearl-gray paint on wood, glass panes. Heaven help us if we get a major earthquake, which everyone knows we will. DON'T KID YOURSELF, reads a popular bumper sticker: SHAKE AND BAKE. He begins pulling out the Riedel wineglasses shaped like opened tulips, their terrifyingly thin walls throwing opalescence, little rainbows sliding over each surface as you turned it in the light. They were a gift from friends—no doubt a frank hint to us that we should upgrade. But the Riedels, like a great deal of other costly crap, are something we'd never buy, given my track record with glass. Neil must be thinking this too, because he stops mid-motion, puts the Riedels back and extracts their sturdier shelf-mates, large bowls on stems. These he holds loosely upside-down in one hand, stems between fingers. With the free hand he plucks each and stands it at attention along the dining table.

"It dawned on me that day, the day of Mamie, there would naturally be others," Neil says. He begins taking serving spoons from a drawer, piling them with a clatter beside the glasses.

"Many others," he says. "And after that—I guess bumping into Mamie sort of opened the door for him—Mike began talking to me about them. Freely. Jubilantly. *The world is her oyster* were the words he always used, waving his hand, every time I tried to object to one or another. To what he was doing."

Neil's voice has thinned to a sort of soft pleading. It's how he talks when he's prefacing tricky material.

"Rae, you know how men can be. It's difficult—"

Deffacahlt indeed.

"—Been that way for so long. I don't love it any more than you do. Mike assumed that because we were men—och, it was understood—you just shagged anything that moved."

I say nothing, washing red butter lettuce, placing the dripping leaves in the colander to drain. The only sound is the stream of cold water from the tap.

"But there was more to it than that," Neil says after a moment. "What confused me was that Mike seemed—well, to *minister* to the women. I think, in his mind, it was more like a cheerful service to them, a generosity?"

I nod at the lettuce, sheafs of red-green sequins under the tap.

"Naturally I couldn't say ennathin," Neil says.

"Naturally," I say.

From the corner of my eye I see his hands lift and open to the ceiling, a gesture American drivers often use to express to a passing driver, *What in the fuck are you doing.*

"Couldn'a object, Rae, without sounding like some sort of old woman. And in those days, for so long, remember, I was on me own."

I watch the leaves in my hands, silky-wet and cold: then steal a peek at Neil's face. He's made no secret of the series of girlfriends he ran through before we met, some of them simultaneous. Each brought, as if to a diabolical potluck, a different flavor of disaster. Fights, sulks, stalemates. Locks were changed, wine flung in faces, gunned engines screeched off in the middle of the night. All very youthful, very urgent. Having lived through my own share of such scenes, I certainly couldn't claim superiority. (I remember chasing a man down the street, weeping, wearing nothing but a kimono.) Like a vaccine each of us has to take, the years of that—I was only a bit ahead of Neil in line. Poor Neil hadn't had much chance to learn better: He'd grown up with a brother, reared on the big-breasted, sneering women on front pages of tabloids. (Stan's a pharmacist, still a bachelor, still living in Glasgow, still dully resentful of his brother's defection—I mean, emigration.) Somehow the more beautiful the women Neil dated, the nastier things got. Most were small-time gold diggers, as best I can tell: his shambling seriousness must have drawn them, his musical accent, nice job. Convinced they could correct him, remodel him, they managed to make him feel bad about everything. Told him he didn't dress right or earn enough money or know the right people. A vasectomy resulted in part from the relentlessness of these determinations: his choice, also in part from the serial horrors of being held hostage by that many late menstrual periods. (The question of children was, thankfully, past for me. That is, I'd wished very hard for them during two precise intervals, ages twenty-seven and thirty-four, but without a compliant mate could only let time move me through those anguished zones like Ulysses lashed to the mast. By the time Neil and I met that great suffering was finished, on top of which I was at the far edge of the fertility curve, and had no desire to be the oldest, tiredest mother in the soccer pool.)

One of his women tried to get him to play golf—which never mind the game was invented in Scotland; he'd always thought it stupid. "If I want to walk around on some grass, I can fecking well go find some grass to walk on." And when he insisted on putting enough gasoline in the clueless women's cars to lift the needle past EMPTY, or if he went searching for an air pump to fill their flattened bike tires, or suggested a firm hour for dinner and assumed they would be ready, they accused him of controlling, of lacking spontaneity. Still, when we began to date I worried. I was nowhere near as beautiful as those women, and for quite some time I couldn't not fear that the next hottie to show up might whisk him off.

Sometimes, at the beginning, I got jealous of the way he looked at women. It felt like a terrible sickness all through me when it came on, worse than retching. I learned quickly what types drew him, began to notice them before he did. Perky, made-up dolls. Nail polish, heels, clingy ensembles. Biggish hair. High-maintenance types—versus me with my black tube skirts and jeans with the fraying hole at the knee, my little jackets, low pumps, touch of mascara, lipstick. I said nothing, mostly. Once or twice we faced off. At a restaurant table I'd watched his eyes lock, and stay locked, on something behind me. I'd waited till I could bear it no longer. Finally I'd murmured, *So what is it about her* to his liquefied eyeballs. My voice must have broken the spell. He'd blinked and I'd watched the filmy coating dissolve: he'd heard me but only barely, regarding me groggily as if I'd waked him. No idea. No least notion. He's taught himself discretion since. Or learned to hide his habits better—maybe that's the same thing. I understand now (absurd, how long it took me): it's all visual with men. The image is oxygen—if not the Lascaux sort, though that may be its ancient antecedent. Anyway, with years, the whole ordeal just sort of faded out. We've outlived so much of our own foolishness—the great, great comfort of age. A fine-looking woman is simply that, no slimy tentacles attached, no stomach-dropping indictment of one's own failure to measure up. Bodies are made differently, and if you received a whole, healthy one when they were handed out, and it's still whole and healthy after four or five decades, you keep going to the gym and taking your vitamins and you shut up about it.

I shake the colander filled with soaked leaves. They lift and fall. Big cold drops rain into the sink.

It took me years to grasp that, compared with the former women, I come out looking like a kind of minor saint. (Actually, it took him years, too.) He used to swear, when I named my worries, that with me he was—honestly, Rae!—so glad to turn the key in the front door any given day, and not dread what awaited him behind it. I loved him for saying that, and I believed him. Still do. But I also understood what he was not saying, what he could never say—out of a sort of crooked gallantry: that he'd been made to relinquish an idea of beauty, of perpetual sexual mystery, that I could never, never supply. And bound into that mystery's heart (truth told) was the flirty taunt, the pouty withholding, the ever-changing costume. The image, in other words, of a prize just-past-reach that spurs men, perfected in magazines and films. He'd been led by it, as have so many, many before him—by the implicit, cruel game, by its advertised barter: *I'm an ice-queen. But if you please me, in ways you're going to have to guess at, I'll fuck you.*

You live with what recedes.

You accommodate, by default.

Time, again, has rescued us: carried us further from the salmon-upstream-thrash. The pretty young admins in his office view him as Papa now. Often they're pregnant, or in the constant, exhausted disarray of raising toddlers. They don't know there was a war in Vietnam, or what Vietnam is, or who Martin Luther King was. "They don't know they were born," Neil likes to snort, though I am sure their looking through him, or past him, makes him wince inside. I remember myself, so clearly and for so long, inhabiting the exact thoughtlessness of those young women. I'd see a white-haired person, man or woman, emerge, say, from the grocery store. And I'd think, casually as breathing, *Why do you still bother? You're as good as dead.*

Now I am thankful, to God or whatever combination of whim and luck drives these currents, for the youngsters' ignoring him. Because if occasion demanded I leave him, I'm almost sure I'd be too tired.

Neil is standing motionless, eyes far away.

"You can imagine the terrible position it put me in," he says. He turns to open the cutlery drawer. The r's in his *terrible* whirl like blades.

I arrange damp leaves in the glass bowl. Light outside has softened, champagne-color. Sunday afternoons hold a deep, peaceable silence.

Neil looks at me.

"Because of course Tilda trusted me as a friend."

"I was Tilda's friend, too. *Am* Tilda's friend," he corrects himself.

He's not looking at me anymore, but into air. As if he's forgotten where he put something, and the act of forgetting unravels him more than the loss of the misplaced thing.

I clap my hands together. "Let's go pick some herbs."

*A*brupt and bracing and welcome, the blueing air out the back door—door that screams like a raptor every time it's opened. I don't oil it, because as much as the sound claws at me I think someday it might announce a burglar—though in truth an intruder could easily enter any of the old back windows while both of us slept sweetly on. "We'll replace these windows soon," Neil mutters as we descend the wood stairs; he is thinking the same thing, which happens more and more these days, and touches me. The skin of my bare arms tightens against the temperature; I should've grabbed a sweater. Sun low, piercing smell of late day, chimney smoke, crushed leaves, cooling earth; aromas of our own pending dinner; of neighbors' dinners. Oh, Sundays! Unbearable time. Implacable stillness. The jay's cry, its flash of blue wing. Tang and clarity that cut, when the nearness of the beloved is about the only thing that keeps you from doubling over.

And Neil's garden: his glory. Testament to the engine of him. Several springs ago he dug two long rectangles, layered in the manure, turned the dark earth. Now one plot hosts a spiky bush of lavender, a baby lime tree, an alarmingly fast-growing fig tree, and a lineup of fading tomatoes that performed bravely before they gasped out. Those straw-like stems in their wire cages yielded up bowl after bowl of glistening heaven—cherries, romas, yellows. Neil would collect them in a Frisbee and, marching into my studio, never mind I was working, hold it out to me: Half-annoyed by the inter-ruption, I'd turn to stick my nose in them, inhale grassy sweetness like hay and sunlight. Some few still hang—red as taillights against the pale stalks and shriveled leaves. In the adjacent plot, bushes of sage, thyme, parsley. I watch Neil stoop to pinch off various bits.

"Yow!" He jerks up, staring at his hand.

"What is it, sweetheart?"

He examines a ruby drop on the pad of his index finger, sticks it in his mouth.

"Fuck," he mumbles around the finger. "Bit of tomato wire sticking out."

"Let me see. When was your last tetanus shot, Neilly?"

"Dunno," he says, re-examining the wet finger, impatient. "Forget it. S'noothin'; be alright."

"It's not *noothin'*." I can't help mock his accent now and again.

I make him show me the puncture, and on impulse, lift his finger to my mouth and enclose it there. I taste grit, salt of his skin, faint iron from the cut.

He looks at me oddly. Smiles a little; gently removes the finger, wipes it on his shirt.

Then he sifts crushed herbs into my hand. I lift the confetti to my nose: Italian, dusty. He surveys his garden, arms folded.

"What's going in next?" I ask.

Neil loves to plan; he'll change his mind twelve times in two hours. My job is to hear out each change, praise the revised idea.

He stares at the plants.

"What about some courgettes?" he murmurs.

Crookneck yellow squash. Delectable with butter, salt, pepper. He knows I adore them. He remembers stuff like this. This, and a thousand other things. He leaves me notes in the morning, every morning, that say *Love You, XX, N.;* beside the words a drawing of a disheveled smiley face wearing a top hat and smoking a pipe, though he never smokes pipes. And never wears hats.

"I would love some courgettes," I say.

I put my arms around him. It seems to me he flinches a moment, then relaxes.

"Neilly, it's fine. It's better than fine. Should we get some mint to put on top of your trifle? And then please can we go back in, sweetheart—I'm freezing!" I shiver against the scratch of his wool shirt.

He lifts my chin, regards me again. The hounded look evanesces, for now.

$\mathcal{T}$he problem of the women would fade for a time, in the story of Mike and Tilda—at least, in Neil's mind it did. All eyes were trained on Addie.

At eighteen she'd won a full scholarship to California Polytechnic, precocious in her studies (to no one's surprise); graduated with high honors. Mike and Tilda drove down to San Luis Obispo for the event, looking more like two aging panhandlers than a college graduate's parents: Mike in his trademark aloha shirt, this one turquoise printed with small brown ukuleles and red hibiscus, the damp cigarette threatening to unstick from the lower lip; by then he carried a paunch the size that gets men hired as Santas. They took Addie and three of her friends—she had made so many friends—to lunch, a Thai restaurant. They stood on the wooden bridge, admired the river that tumbled prettily through town. They shook hands with Addie's teachers, who raved what an ideal student she'd been, fresh air, a classroom joy. Mike brought along a half-dozen black mollies in clear, lidded bowls as gifts. He'd given the matter careful thought: the mollie worked best because of its peaceful nature, and because it adapts readily to either fresh or saltwater. He made the others wait while he took recipients aside for instructions in the mollies' care. The parties posed for photographs on the grass in the June sun: age-spotted, flabby and creased Mike and Tilda flanking the radiant young woman in her black gown, blonde locks shining beneath her tasseled mortarboard. Addie had become what was called, in my own youth's heyday, a knockout. In the photos she holds her mother and father tightly around their shoulders, taller by over a head than both of them, grinning. (She still had the lovely habit of scrunching up her shoulders when she laughed.) Neil posed the groups, snapping pictures: Of course Mike and Tilda had dragged him along for the occasion; he was relieved, he says, to have something useful to do.

"You seem to have functioned as a kind of best man to the Spenders' entire lives," I say to him now, very gently.

Neil sighs, tossing the dishtowel over his shoulder.

"I knew them first," he says, shrugging. "Mike was my first American friend. Also," he adds a bit testily, "Mike saved my life, if you want to get technical."

I assume he means his drubbing in the waters off French Polynesia. Would he have died there, clinging to Mike's little boat? I know better than to debate that just now.

I also know better than to laugh.

He opens the refrigerator, removes his hors d'oeuvres. Smoked oysters, marinated vegetables, tzatziki, olives, sliced salami from Viviani's (the serious, expensive deli), Pecorino Romano cheese, and (I am guessing) as a memory-lane treat for Mike, a pile of foil-wrapped wedges of Vache Qui Rit—the American version, Laughing Cow. Same cartoon on the label, same red cow's mirthful face, same hoop earrings the shape of the round container of wedges. Mike won't be able to open those wedges by himself—Neil surely knows that. No doubt Tilda will do it. Or one of us. Perhaps Neil just wants to help Mike remember.

He places the food on the wooden island, arranging the silver-foiled wedges into a little mandala. Begins cutting the Pecorino.

"After that," he says as he works, "things seemed to be ticking over. At least on the face of it."

Addie went to work within a year of graduation, apprenticing with Oceanside Engineering, a progressive young firm in Mira Flores. She took to it at once, a proud duckling on water: scouted sites, measured and recorded, photographed sidewalks, pavement, signage, railroad tracks. She wrote letters, produced calculations, compiled reports—chores given to those called, with real affection, *baby engineers*. She attended after-work seminars in Seismic Review. She went to lecture banquets, toured visitors, chose Christmas cards, planned company parties, arranged copies of *Safety & Industrial Essentials* and *OpFlow* and *ENR* on the break room table. Addie loved all of it. Her bosses, a cartel of five married men, conducted themselves with a kind of sorrow in her presence, because her beauty was close to frightening. Something about the combination of blonde hair with dark brown eyes, dark brows.

These effects didn't take long to bring on the inevitable. One day in early spring Addie drove with three of her co-workers on a survey run for the eventual laying of drainage pipe. There she stood, erect and vigilant in the trampled wheat, backlit like a Monet. But in place of a frosting-colored gown and parasol, she wore jeans and an orange hard hat and chartreuse day-glo vest with red velcro fasteners, bearing down on that surveyor's rod as if she had a dragon pinned beneath it.

A young planner from the county water agency (working with Addie's firm on the project) drove to the grassy site for his lunch break. It wasn't far from the river; the air smelled of freshwater moss, and new green. From a distance of perhaps 100 feet he spied the blonde sentry at her post. She was frowning, awaiting instructions from her colleagues, who paced the field at some distance from her, pausing to converse.

That is how Chet told it to Neil, when they finally met.

Chet turned off the engine. He whistled through his teeth, a long, fading note.

His partner, Frank, drowsed against the passenger window chewing his ham-and-cheese.

"Hm?"

"I don't know who she is," Chet said, without taking his eyes from the girl.

"But I am going to marry her."

Afternoon light warmed the truck cab, which smelled of ham sandwiches, apple cores (browning on the cab floor), coffee, steam of the men's breath. Outside the air was soft and still. Slips of first wildflowers peeped through the long grass, blue and yellow like miniature orchids. Frank laughed around a mouthful of sandwich as he rolled down his window. As he did the tender air floated in, quickening in the men's nostrils and ears, a scent like fresh cream.

"Sure you are, Prince Charming." Frank said, yawning. "And I'm the Easter Bunny."

❧

CHET EPHRAIM Lockhart married Astrid Louise Spender at the popular Windemere winery, set in vineyard-combed hills half an hour northeast of Mira Flores.

Tilda by then poured for Windemere's tasting room (they asked few questions about employee pasts); she had talked the principals into a bargain rental fee for the event. It was a hot, clear Sunday in June, 2003—one year after Addie's graduation. She was twenty-three; Chet twenty-five.

"Oooh, a wedding. I need *details*, Neil."

I am measuring filtered water into the barrel-shaped glasses. I try to encourage people to drink water at our dinners. But too often the big glasses go ignored; at evening's end I find many standing, lonely and full, amid the emptied bottles, flutes, snifters.

Neil rolls his eyes, squats to search the lower shelves.

"Will ye keep yer knickers on. Where are the dinner napkins?"

"Other side. Men never notice the same stuff women do. I have to cross-examine you. Under the paper plates, on the right."

Eventually I will find a way to see a photo album, which I'm certain will tell me all he won't have noticed. What woman can resist photos? All the tribal tom-toms brought to bear, the clothes, hair, complexions. How ridiculously young everyone looks. Of course fashions date quickly, and film colors sicken. But something's still readable there. Lights in eyes. What people thought they were pointing themselves toward. What woman does not stare and stare, trying to add it up?

Chet was the son of an Idaho potato farmer. He'd struck out early from a family of eight, determined never to look at a potato again except maybe in a steakhouse, and even then only in some extra-fancied-up form. He made Addie love him almost

- 63 -

immediately with his quiet self-possession, the way his eyes followed hers. He had an inverted-triangle head—wide end up—curly brown hair, a peaceful brow, high cheekbones. She loved him, too, for an early story he told about his father. They were standing together on the spaceship home's nubbly lawn, a Saturday morning in May, air like peaches. Chet took her hands.

"One morning," he said, "I watched my dad—he was a small, wiry man who didn't talk much—I watched him go out into the yard with our old electric toaster under his arm, the cord dangling behind it like a tail. It had been burning toast, or not cooking it right. He positioned the toaster on the flat stump we always used for splitting firewood, a little distance from the house. Then he went around the side of the house to his toolshed, came back with the wood axe. I watched him raise the axe and bring it down on the toaster. Two, three times. Dropped the axe, dusted his hands, walked off."

Chet told it with gravity, a near-invisible twitch at the edges of his mouth. Addie stood gazing at him in the clear morning, the breeze lifting strands of her hair. Then something lit in her eyes and she began to laugh and laugh, a sound like silver coins.

Make a woman laugh, my friends, and that's it. Or a great deal of it.

Like Addie, Chet was an engineer. He liked to figure things out, grid projects into numbered tasks, dispatch each with precision, one by one. Mostly, Neil thinks, Chet won Addie with the solemnity that never left his face. As though during the actual minutes he gazed at you he was understanding something beyond joking about. It appeared, in those moments, as if you could dive and dive and never find the bottom of his thinking.

For the ceremony Addie wore a white knee-length shift of raw silk—the fabric threw light—and low white heels. A short veil framed her face when she put it back to kiss her new husband. Beneath it her hair, swept up in a French roll, shone gold.

Frank Jacobsen stood by as best man: shifting from foot to foot, each shaved-raw cheek bulging over his collar. He could not wait to get hold of a drink.

Addie had asked her Uncle Neil to be ring-bearer.

"I was terrified, afraid I'd drop the rings," Neil says, arranging cheese.

"Did you?"

"No. But it was so hot that day, for a minute I thought I'd pass out."

Tilda sat upfront in the family row, mild and collected, while beside her Mike struggled for composure: eyes leaking, lips trembling. He finally lowered his bald head, pressing a wad of tissues (supplied by Tilda) to his face, and from behind you could see his big shoulders and the reddening fat rolls on the back of his neck shake with noiseless weeping. He looked, Neil admits, like a sobbing convict. Others in the audience wept too, but those were mainly older women whose dainty sniffles punctuated the vows. Addie and Chet smiled as they spoke to each other. Behind them, in every direction, the rows of vines wove over the hills to the blue horizon, puffy with new green—leafy protection for small sprays of green or black berries, the size of ball-bearings. The cypress trees that marked out the area pointed heavenward; the sun's warmth seeped from the red earth, and it could have been Tuscany.

Rows and rows of white folding chairs were filled by Tilda's friends from the winery and the town—even some of her former Book Stash colleagues. But most guests came from Mike's prior lives. Had the event been a movie, Neil said, the scene might have made a fitting culmination over which to run credits—a smooth pan-shot over every face: Bikers from the Porthole in wool caps and vests, despite the heat. Abalone divers, creased from sun and salt. An old Tahitian named Kaké Teuru, brown and lined, who'd once worked for the Papeete Airport. Downtown people, neighbors of Finny Business, the luggage guy, the deli guy, the Tibetan artifacts guy. And there was Mike's longtime assistant Ben, lanky, grinning, flanked by a young wife and two bashful children. Old hippies dressed in velvet and slippers, reeking of patchouli; kids racing around, rangy and sticky as gypsies. Addie's pals from high school and Cal Poly: laughing, beautiful. Some had flown in from far away; Addie had booked them at the adjacent Windemere Inn so they could walk back to their rooms. Which meant they'd be able to drink. Which they did, in earnest, with everyone else. Champagne, beer from medical-looking tubes that poked from wood kegs, every manner of wine. Tilda oversaw the caterers; cooked up a pile herself. A United Nations of food: chow fun, dim sum, empanadas, pyramids of shrimp and cocktail sauce, cheeses, salmon and steak, fluffy pieces of cake. Then came rock music, and bride and groom opened the dance portion, sexily, with "Beast of Burden." Then everyone else danced including the little kids, and it was bedlam as the scarlet sun melted, and the air, cooling, went peacock blue. As light waned and action became impenetrable, Neil saw Addie's honey-colored arm reach through a wall of bouncing bodies to grasp the hand of her father, who'd been standing outside the spectacle like a lost bear. Again, as if it were a movie, the crowd parted, music slowed, and Addie danced with Mike to "Sunrise, Sunset."

"Oh, sweetheart."

I hug myself. I'm stupid for weddings.

"It *was* something." Neil nods. He turns from me a moment, but I can see the hasty wrist push at the corners of his eyes.

Chet and Addie honeymooned in Cabo San Lucas, where the Spenders had once—how long ago it must have seemed, yet perhaps also not so very long—camped in their old VW bus, and where the urchin Addie had run fearlessly along the beach, toting pieces of seaweed and polished bottle glass, singing.

"May I ask where Mike and Tilda found the money for all this?"

Neil is sorting the cutlery.

He cocks his head, makes a face.

"Guess."

I consider. "Mike's ma."

"Well *done*, lassie."

Where else, I am thinking, would the money come from? Addie's fine brains got her school and a job, but a big wedding and honeymoon—high ticket. Then I think of something else. I stand with my back to the sink.

"Neil, how come Mike's ma didn't make it to the wedding?"

"She was dead."

I put a hand to the counter, though I do not feel surprised, or sad. More like watching a coin fall and roll and drop soundlessly, neatly, into an inaccessible drain. I let the moment flit by. An old woman, a life. A little breeze between one's ears. Though something back of conscious thought whispers: *And when it's your turn, when you are the one mentioned this way? A moment's breeze, someone's dim, fleet recollection.* I can't even remember Mike's mother's name.

"I can't remember her name," I say softly.

Neil sighs. "Louise."

"What happened to Louise's estate, then?"

Neil looks at me, wiping his hands.

"They spent it all. Every last dime."

"What?" I am trying to follow. "They who?"

"Mike and Tilda, cloth-ears! Who else d'you imagine?"

Dumb wonder. "Spent it—doing what?"

Travel. While Addie was at college in San Luis, Tilda took an unpaid leave from her winery job. They went to New Orleans, Hawaii, Miami, Las Vegas. Fancy hotels. Ate and drank like rajahs.

They frittered the fucking money completely away.

They should have bought a house, I am thinking. Fools, fools. I hardly know whether I've said the words or thought them. You have to understand what homes cost here now. It would have given them retirement, something to pass on to Addie. It seems I have spoken, because Neil answers briskly.

"Not a concern—at least not for Addie," he says, hanging the towel. He bends to eye the window in the oven door.

Chet's company, with four partners, was taking rapid command—city budgets replenished themselves like wells—all over the Southwest. Addie wore a new ring, a circle of diamonds, next to her wedding ring, and the Lockharts purchased a villa named Rancho Dorado.

"Man," I say, swallowing. Except for the gold band from Avignon, I don't wear jewelry. I buy wire earrings from a turnstile in the sundries section of the drugstore. And Neil won't wear rings. He fears industrial accidents, factory machinery, though of course he's worked all his adult life in an office. Another byproduct of the Dickensian childhood.

"But then the curtain fell," Neil is saying.

He shakes his head.

"Oh aye, Rae. The worst, when it happened. Which no one had prepared me for. Not in all those years," he mutters, staring at the pile of knives.

"What no one bothered to keep track of—what no one even bothered to mention—was the state of Mike's health."

He sounds angry but also puzzled, lost in wonder.

To look useful I begin folding napkins. Light through the window has turned blue. Outside a dove flutters, with its soft *brrr* of startlement, to a rooftop. There are two of them—doves—out there; I see them together every afternoon. Gentle, poised, never apart. I love seeing the pair of them scuttling around in Neil's garden blithe as air, heads bobbing forward, poking at his clover—though they must surely be prey to a half-dozen neighborhood cats.

"Every bad thing you could have," Neil is saying, "Mike had."

And everything you could do wrong, he did, by long habit. High blood pressure. Overweight. Smoked "every hour God sent," as Neil puts it. Never dreamed of slowing down, and if anyone had suggested it, would have squashed that idea the way he stubbed out a smoke butt. Mike was one of those who hate doctors; never saw one if he could help it, ever. He'd buck and paw away any hand that tried to smear a dab of sunscreen on him. Ate all the wrong stuff, the vein-clogging, heart-stopping stuff. No exercise—quit diving when Addie was born. The times he put on a wetsuit and bodysurfed in the freezing bay were too few to count. Of course he and Tilda had been drinking like fiends from the start. Worst, Mike's father had died early of a stroke, when Mike was barely grown. If the father crumps of a stroke—so goes the medical lore—the son is extra-susceptible. Regular folks assume, touchingly, that if a son *knows* this, why, of course he will be extra vigilant.

Neil ponders the cheese slices as if they might rearrange themselves to form a message.

"Tilda hired a private investigator," he says abruptly.

The fact of the P.I., hired in 2004, became known to Neil, like much else, far later. For a long period, please understand, he did not know—nobody knew—how the series of events that followed, domino-style, had been triggered.

Neil learned eventually. So that, at least, looking back on what came next made a sick sort of sense. True: after a number of years any adult paying attention tends to loosen all notions of sense. The older we get, the more media headlines sound like hooting satire: sex, war, money. It lowers the bar—it nullifies the bar—for shock, for violation, and at some point the mind balks. Yet (bravely, idiotically) the mind persists in its longing for sense: habit-trained like an old dog to search for anything meaningful in its dish. Again and again we nose the familiar bowl. We turn on the television, open a newspaper, a book. We ask someone how they are, and really want to know.

Not rational. But neither is any human act of faith, having a baby, falling in love.

Marrying.

As one woman, a novelist friend, once put it to me, laughing: *Oh, Rae. What else is there to do?*

TILDA HAD of course understood, throughout Addie's growing up, that Mike was out hound-dogging. It takes no genius on a woman's part to sense such things, and aside from the care of his beloved stock, Mike was not a man you'd call fastidious. Tilda may have literally smelled it. Women smell everything, know it in their bodies before their minds do. Doubtless Mike came home late, unfindable much of the time. He may've wafted a foreign scent. She may have tripped over scraps and tokens, with or without meaning to. Stains, receipts, phone calls that clicked off when she answered. Women know.

After Addie moved to Albuquerque, where Chet headquartered his partnership, Tilda and Mike left the spaceship house to its befuddled landlord, gave away or trashed their belongings (most too shabby to sell) and resettled, with the now-arthritic old Bud, into a cheap apartment rental in town: a one-bedroom near a small children's park. Mike's mother was not dead yet, and the two had to scrape, as usual, for money. Tilda kept her tasting room job, which meant an hour's drive north in Dottie Datsun. (The van had long ago been sold for scrap; Dottie's engine had been replaced.) Mike could now walk to Finny Business, which, despite the downtown's changes, had hung on. (Many old-timers believed Mike had cut a deal with the building's owner to keep his store's rent low, which likely involved a reliable supply of decent-grade marijuana.) Still a huge man but sallower and saggier, Mike remained irrepressible, plotting new stock—he'd arranged to acquire a small shark, convinced it would become the store's big draw; word of mouth still worked fast in the county. He still wandered the street bullshitting people all day, a *boulevardier* of the big, odorous kind. (Mike smelled, in those years, like a man who has been doing heavy, physical work. Say what you will, women liked it.) Younger generations nodded at Mike on the street: they had no quarrels with the whacked-out old local dude. They admired his irreverence, a kind of street theater. If you drove down Main you could still most often find him in front of the store, entertaining tourists (by then infiltrating the region, exuberant with discovery). You could hear his great *HA!* for a full block, even through closed windows. Posing for photos, kissing babies, handing out tokens (keychains, plastic drink-stirrers in the shapes of bettas) as if he were, as usual, running for office.

And Tilda hired a detective, from San Francisco. We'll never know how she found money to pay him. Maybe she arranged an installment plan. More probably, Neil guesses, she traded her debt in bulk wine, which she obtained at little or no cost. She did not volunteer details, and Neil, stricken, could never bring himself to ask. She did finally tell Neil the detective's name: Hoyt Chandler. She offered—the same complacent way she'd once said *Five finger discount*—that she'd found Chandler in the San Francisco phone book. (The detective's name sounded bogus to me, like an actor's or porn star's.)

She told Neil she had wanted someone from away, from outside the county. Someone known by no one here. She hired Chandler a year after Addie left for New Mexico. Mike was fifty-four.

I'll remind you now what Tilda looked like, as long as I knew her. She was built square. Always shuffling around in a man's shirt and trousers, hair bowl-cut, not often washed, her breath awful, face roseate and squinty as if it had suffered too much outdoor exposure. Despite or maybe because of these elements you looked twice at Tilda, and then you looked away. Some toughened, wiseacre air about her, marinated in the brine of life, a sort of smug leer, discomfited the onlooker. She sweat a lot no matter what the season; this, with her breath and the network of infinitesimal red veins on her face, signaled she'd been drinking all day. Small, steady sips. Of course the tasting room job lent itself magnificently to this habit, though technically it was illegal. But Tilda drank every day. And the drink loosened her tongue.

"All I have is what she told me," Neil says. He twists an old cork off the corkscrew.

Tilda first met with Chandler at a café called the Breakaway, during lunch hour on a Wednesday in March. She couldn't receive the detective at home; Mike might stop in for food or some gizmo for the store he'd forgotten, or to check the mail because he was bored. Nor could she consider meeting in town, because Mike owned the downtown, roved it all day like an oversized mascot. The Breakaway was a rest-stop, a café-grocery off the two-lane highway through the vineyards. On weekdays the place stayed quiet, exempting vacation periods and summer. Bicyclists liked to pause there in the middle of long treks; a few Hell's Angels, some tourists. You could get a sandwich or salad and sit at one of the cement tables outside if weather was good; if not you could sit inside. Since it was cold and windy out, she sent Chandler to a back corner indoors, one of the small wire tables and chairs. His meaty hind parts seemed to overpower the chair. She sat opposite, her hands around a glass of beer into which she dashed, before his eyes, a long shot of tequila from a flask removed from her tote bag.

"Mexican cocktail," she said.

Chandler took black coffee.

Early March, overcast light. A season we know well, of course. Rows and rows of vines comb the hills, sleeping all the way to the horizon, a vast cemetery of dark bare crucifixes twining their stakes and espaliers. Not many people were about that day; some few pushed through the screen door at the front, tinkling the old-fashioned bell. The corner where Tilda and Chandler sat was lit by a fluorescent tube bolted to the ceiling; it gave them both a blueish, drugstore caste. Visitors ordering lunches up front made an effective sound curtain, but the two kept their voices low.

Tilda looked Chandler over. He was a middle-aged man with yellowish skin, pouches beneath his eyes underscored by greenish-brown lines. Thin hair, teeth dark from cigarettes, fingertips too. But his gray eyes were awake and crisp. This pleased Tilda. He asked questions, removed a ballpoint from his jacket pocket, scribbled notes in an ordinary five-and-dime spiral pad.

"I know what he's doing," Tilda told the detective simply. "I've known a long, long time. But I want photographs. Dates, and places."

Chandler nodded, scribbling. Did she also, he asked, want contact information for the "co-respondents," as he called them.

She thought a moment. "No. Fuck 'em."

Then her eyebrows lifted, her smile dry.

"Well, and he did!"

She took a swallow of beer, raised her eyes again to Chandler's. Her manner was composed, pleasant.

"He'd fuck a snake if he could figure out a way to hold it still long enough."

That was in March, according to what Tilda told Neil.

By May Chandler had phoned her at the tasting room, as she'd instructed, and told her he was ready to meet. This time the Breakaway wouldn't work, he said. Tilda found a bar by a gas station off the old northbound highway, decrepit and dark. She drove there from the winery in midafternoon. (Because she could jolly her customers, knew wine, and showed up when other employees disappeared, Tilda had been made manager of the Windemere tasting room; she could dictate her own shifts.) She was waiting for Chandler when he arrived. Three tables and a bar, with no one around that hour but the lone tender who polished glasses, fixated on the basketball game on television above the bar. The place smelled like all the others of its kind, stale beer, faint ammonia of urine, aftershave fumes of well-pours. Lit inside as if within a muddy river. It appeared to suit Chandler, who stopped a moment in the doorway, scanned the room, nodded, and entered.

The photographs he fanned on the table like a card deck, without comment, were black and white, eight by ten. He lit a cigarette. Then (though she did not ask) he lit one for Tilda, passed it to her, sat back. His face had nothing to say. Behind him a gymnasium audience shrieked; giant black men lunged and leapt in sweating herds; bullhorns honked, furious whistles blew. Tilda said nothing as she studied the photos, picking absently at a corner of one of them. With the other hand she sucked from the cigarette Hoyt had handed her, puffing the smoke off quickly to the side, her eyes on the photos yet seeming also to look through them, or past them. The bad light made the photos dimmer, their blown-up images grainier. One showed Mike from the rear, nude, kneeling on a bed at the feet of the prone nude body of what appeared to be a middle-aged woman with dark-dyed hair, whose features wore (as best you could tell) an insensate expression. The smudged shape of a bottle was discernible on a table by the bed. Edges and surfaces diffused, as if their molecules were coming apart. Mike's ass and legs had hair all over them, which in the blow-ups looked like fur.

"Jesus Christ."

I've pulled out a dining chair and, seated before Neil's armada of wineglasses, I look at my hands—they are freezing, though the house isn't cold—fingers meshed as if I am about to plead for clemency, or sing in church. I rub them, run them through my hair, plug them into my armpits. The doves outside have ceased burring; silence in the kitchen makes an electric hum. The stove clicks, a brief hiss inside of cooking potatoes and lamb.

Rosemary, garlic.

Our little house, our little life.

Neil looks at the clock. He pulls another chair from the table, folds his long form into it and leans back, ankles crossed, hands behind his head.

"About that time, y'see, the baby came."

$\mathcal{G}$eneral Hospital, Albuquerque, New Mexico. Under white lights amid boxes of metal, beeping gauges and tubes, surrounded by buzzing humans in green scrubs whose eyes watched a shaved and sore vagina isolated and transformed by draped sheets into a small spotlighted flesh-cave: from between its walls of blood-flecked straining, in whitish-paste-and-blood-covered sections, one giving onto the next with a sound like a muffled cougar cub when the last of him was out, emerged an enraged Harrison Michael Lockhart.

Harry was a hard-packed baby, his wet body working and crimson as if he'd been fighting the entire term of his compaction in utero as well as his exit from it; Addie had a mighty job of pushing him out. In photos her grin is lopsided, hair dark with sweat; one arm hoists the swaddled red bomb, lurid against the flower-print billow of her hospital gown. Early snaps show an infant (once he'd unclenched) capped to the brow in a sock like a tiny burglar, frowning in sleep, arms folded Khrushchev-style under his swaddling—a virtual copy of photos of the baby Mike Spender. (Addie had secured those for safekeeping, years back, from her Grandma Louise.) Except unlike baby Mike, baby Harry had arrived with a perfectly coiffed mass of wavy black hair—as if lifted from a miniature matinee idol's head. And his eyes were not Mike's brown-black but copies of Chet's: crisp blue, filled with appraising smoke and, as both his parents soon learned, unrelenting.

Chet and Addie stepped up to all of it: the sleeplessness, diapers, wipes, creams, baths, laundries, vaccinations, feedings, wakings, voidings, inscrutable alternations of peace and screaming—with vivid preference, on the baby's part, for screaming. Both parents felt as though they were being pounded systematically by some gigantic mortar and pestle, pounded day and night until they'd been rendered into something whey-like, a byproduct with neither wits nor will. Dazed, awed by the ferocious package of flesh which they had somehow themselves elicited and now ruled their lives, they prepared to fly with Harry to show him to Mike and Tilda, as soon as doctors gave the okay.

"The next thing I remember is the call from paramedics," Neil says.

He has turned the dining chair backward and straddles it, facing me.

The oven's fragrant load hisses. The house holds still.

The phone had burst open his sleep. He blinked, struggled to focus at the clock. Very late, a starless Saturday night in May. It was, he remembered, Memorial Day weekend: everyone gone for the three-day holiday. Streets had emptied; even the freeway becalmed.

Medics had found Neil's phone number in Mike's wallet.

"That's always meant a lot to me," Neil says.

This abrades me. Why should Neil be touched Mike kept his number handy? Who else had put up with Mike so consistently, for so long? Who else bailed him from jams so repeatedly, so faithfully, demanding nothing back?

I stay silent.

No one answered the phone at Mike's home, which the cops tried first. Because Addie's number was a long distance area code, and because her last name was not written on the slips in Mike's wallet, the cops couldn't immediately know she was a relative. (Town had by then transfigured into City, countless officers, dispatch personnel, many commuting in from other cities. Gone the days of everyone knowing everyone.)

The cops tried Neil's number next.

"Rae, I canna tell ye how dreadful it was."

Neil's brogue always gets thicker in distress. He has tucked his chin over the chair back, looking at the floor. I reach without thinking to pat his head and notice a pink patch of scalp at the back of the crown, amazed I've not noticed it before. The naked clearing seems a secret vulnerability, a wearing-away unknown to Neil while he was giving best attention to others. It makes me want to open my whole being like a raincoat and wrap him. With care not to startle him, I cup a hand to the nape of his neck.

He doesn't look up.

"When you've known someone that long," he says to the linoleum, "after a point it can't matter anymore how crazy they are."

Grandfathered in, he used to say.

Neil threw on his clothes that night and rushed to Finny Business, but the ambulance had left for the hospital by the time he got there. Police were everywhere, flashing cars pulled sideways blocking both ends of the street, filling what would have normally been a black and silent, buttoned-down night with the red-white-blue lights that blinded, and hypnotized. The air cackled and squawked with radio voices: hocking, clicking, scraping sounds. The medics had tipped the cops that Neil was a first contact, and the distracted cops led him through the yellow tape outside, cordoning off the store.

One of the cops recognized Neil from court. The cop nodded at him, but warned him not to leave: they would have to question him. At the line of yellow tape across the sidewalk a group of passersby had assembled, whomever happened to be wandering around that late, teenaged skateboarders, bums; one pushed a shopping cart under the early morning stars.

Though Neil was never religious, he remembers he wanted to genuflect when he stepped through the door of Finny Business.

"Don't walk in here," one cop said, angry and quick. It was then Neil looked down and saw (still waking in that untoward hour, the whole tableau a rococo dream) that he was standing in water. The cops moving through the place, making notes, taking photos, were wearing blue neoprene waders—what he'd called Wellies as a child, only much heavier. The blue boots moving through water and broken glass made sounds, *splish-clink, splish-clink*. Like an aftermath, Neil thought, of an earthquake, or hurricane. Water drained over the doorsill onto the walk, into the half-lit dark.

The stink was algous, humid. Water inches deep, carpet a murk beneath, and in the water and above it, pieces of glass festooned with glistening green ropes of plants like entrails. Twined or tossed from the plants, little bodies, some bleeding, some shivering as the life left them. Mollies, parrot fish, eels, catfish, bettas, angels. The clown loach, the honey gouramis, the rosy barb, loved by Addie as a kid because it resembled the goldfish Cleo in *Pinocchio*. Many so tiny you didn't see them until the edge of your vision caught a twitch, or spasm. Mike's prize dwarf shark, its showcase tank in ruins, hunched in the rubble like a stiff coat shoved off a chair. Under the fluorescent glare the poor creatures lay gasping or twitching, some leaking blood. One or two shivered and leapt in a final, aerial arc, as much as a couple of feet. As they died their eyes went from shock to vacancy, and their shining opalescent flesh flattened to gray.

A sulfuric reek: boxes on the floor of freeze-dried worms, brine shrimp and vegetable flakes, water-treatment chemicals, had been soaked through and were expanding sponge-like through sogged cardboard. Where the fish tanks had stood grinned the remnants of many giant mouths of knocked-out teeth, a serrated series of glass terraces over the frames and shelving that had supported them.

Every tank in the store had been smashed.

Splish-clink, splish-clink. The cops not writing or taking pictures wore bright yellow rubber gloves as they moved, though they did not seem to be touching anything.

Neil found his voice to ask one of the cops, who'd paused to request he back out of the store lest he get hurt, how it had been done.

"Baseball bat," said the cop. "No prints. Gloves, probably." The assailant had left the bat behind and run off, once outside.

That was how the cop said it: *assailant*. They got no footprints. It was likely, they said, that cheap drugstore galoshes had been worn inside the store, which would have no markings or even a seam on the soles; any markings dried by the time the cops got there, the asphalt retaining no discernible print. The galoshes had probably, said the cop, been removed outside. "Probably threw 'em into a car and peeled outta here," he said. No witnesses, yet.

When the officers squared off with him Neil could only confirm he was Mike's friend. He didn't dare volunteer more.

He asked—meekly—where Mrs. Spender was.

"Getting off her shift at the winery, on her way now." To his surprise, they did not ask him more about Tilda. When instead they asked, looking hard at him, *Any idea who may have done this? Spender have any enemies you knew of?*—the word *enemy* struck Neil's ears as laughably, fussily quaint, like the word *sarsparilla*. He didn't have to draw on a lifetime of courtroom hours to make his face impenetrable: he'd known nothing at the time, remember, of the private detective. Beneath his careful demeanor, though, some sickening sense worked his bowels—he had to excuse himself to void them in the mall bathroom, accompanied by one of the officers and the squinting old security guard who provided the key. Once he'd returned the cops continued to interrogate him, searching his face. Finally, their own fatigue took over.

"Thanks, Mr. Abercrombie. We'll be in touch. Remember to notify us if you plan to leave town."

Neil raced to Memorial Hospital.

The police had told him, but only when he asked, what the ambulance personnel had radioed back: Mike had suffered a massive stroke.

It took Neil the drive time to the hospital (hands prickling with adrenalin, clasping the wheel) to review the night's sequence piece by piece. He walked himself through what the cops had told him, as if relearning the alphabet. Mike had been summoned to the scene by a phone call from the cops, who had in turn been alerted by the alarm system company that Finny Business had been entered. (By that time, the downtown ran a strict merchant association; each member was required by insurance to fully wire his premises.)

"Mr. Spender? You'd better come over to your shop immediately, sir. Yes, sir: right now, please. There's been an, uh—an incident."

Whoever had entered had used a key, but had not known how to punch in the code that disarmed the alarm system. Tilda had the Spenders' only car at her winery shift. Mike would have run—as best Mike could approximate running—the twelve blocks to the shop (his great belly boinging and shuddering in front of him: the image made Neil wince). Cops would have been cordoning off the scene when Mike staggered up, sweating and heaving. They'd have escorted him to the threshold of the entrance, stopped him there.

"Mr. Spender, we can't let you go in any further just yet."

Mike, still struggling for air, would have stared at the wreckage, the soaked boxes, stranded garlands of wet plants, glass shards, pale flesh, blood, rank steam. In seconds he began murmuring, sounds that were not words. He swayed, his head lolled; he gripped his head with both hands and the murmurs became screams; his features clenched. His legs gave way and he crumpled, screaming that he was going blind.

"The police never found enough evidence to indict anyone," Neil says.

He considers his laced hands, hanging hammock-like below the chair back on which he's propped his chin.

"They questioned some people. No one they could ever pin it on. No witnesses either—at least none who'd come forward."

I do not ask—and Neil has not offered—how much he may have had to do with this fact, or whether at that point in the city's history he *could* have had anything to do with it. I doubt he could. Burglaries, he reminds me, were routine by those years, vandalism, carjacking, shootings. The papers bristled with accounts, far more serious—drug busts, gang wars, kidnappings—pushing the ante to that weary point in a burgeoning city's police force when it is all the cops can do to keep track, never mind solve.

Mike's attack had been ischemic, meaning that a clot blocks blood flow to the brain. The stroke had occurred in the left side of his brain. He did not in fact go blind, but the right half of his body and left side of his face were paralyzed.

Finny Business was a complete loss. To Neil's sorrow (but not surprise), Mike had not insured the store well. Impossible to recoup the capital needed to replace it.

The most immediate crisis was finding money to sustain a crippled Mike.

He would receive a pitiful amount of disability, time limited, and a small social security stipend. Overnight he and Tilda became dependent on her income from the tasting room, which came nothing near (in Tilda's words) "an adult salary"; though in sympathy for her new hardship Windemere gave her a couple of weeks' paid time off, and increased her hourly wage by a dollar. Neil thanked every god in heaven Tilda had had the wits to enroll herself and Mike in a medical plan the winery offered, which included generic drugs. Addie and Chet pledged a generous check every month. But even after Mike had learned to walk, excruciatingly, with a cane, and to speak, also with agonizing slowness—the Spenders' mail slot bled bills. Specialized drugs, physical therapy (only partially covered by insurance, time-limited). Oh, the clauses, disclaimers, the resistance; the erroneous bills! The wheelchair, the braces and bandages, the special seat Tilda had to set up for Mike in the shower. At the beginning she had to clean him, prop him, help him shit. After he was semi-mobile and could mostly feed himself, Tilda tried to have all his food, drink and meds apportioned and laid out within easy reach before she left for work each morning: toilet paper rolled into grabbable pads, jazz station on low, sliding glass door open a crack to the concrete patio—everything at the ready. She hurried between home and work every day lest he may have fallen, dropped something, or worse.

Neighbors in the apartment complex said it wasn't that they were not sorry, but didn't working people have the right to a peaceable home? They could not bring themselves to meet Tilda's eyes when they saw her driving off in the morning; it tore at their sleep, made them angry, that ragged voice calling half the night in slurred syllables:

TIL-DA.

The first night, Neil stayed alongside Tilda in the hospital room with the unconscious Mike until the nurses threw them both out. The second night Tilda drove home to shower and change, but Neil slept on a couch in the waiting room, taking what he calls a swill (splashing the upper half of himself at a sink) in the hospital restroom, reappearing in Mike's room next morning. This went on for a week. He asked his office partners to cover hearings and take on work that could not be postponed;

instructed his admins to reschedule all appointments. In Mike's room he and Tilda said almost nothing to each other, but both spoke encouragingly to Mike. While Mike slept they dozed, tried to read, stared out the window or at nothing.

Neil was still there with her when Addie, Chet and Harry arrived.

Addie appeared first in the doorway, holding Harry. They had dressed him in blue corduroy overalls, his now-brown hair flowering above. Addie, in a chocolate jumpsuit and pearls, looked thinner, her cheekbones more pronounced. She stepped at once to her father, squatting beside him on low heels, held the infant close to Mike's face. One of her hands propped the baby's torso and head; the other hand cupped his bottom. Harry's smoke-blue eyes looked everywhere, his hands like pink stars fisting.

Luckily for the entire hospital floor, the baby was relatively calm that morning.

"Daddy?" Addie said.

"This is Harry, Daddy."

Mike's eyes opened wide, pored over the baby's skin, his celebrity hair, eyes ricocheting to follow forms, lights. Mike looked back to Addie, his own eyes filling. His mouth worked on one side, saliva collecting there. He blinked twice by way of thanking her. Tears coursed down his cheeks, and also down Addie's, while the baby's excited gaze shot around the room, small fists opening, closing.

Tilda, crying, came forward, took the baby from Addie and began to nuzzle and whisper to him. Addie leaned over her prone father, put both her arms around him, and wept against his useless right arm.

Chet came into the room then, and he and Neil shyly shook hands.

ut Neil!"

I stare around the kitchen, steeped in shadow. I want to fill my chest with air; it feels petrified, clamped tight.

"How did Tilda act while you were with her in the hospital room? Didn't you notice anything? Didn't you *say* anything?"

Neil stands, stretches, rubs his hands against the sides of his pants as if to gain back the feel in them.

"Rae, I wasn't thinking about such things. Remember I knew nothing of the detective business then. All I remember is—well, shock. Stupidity. We hardly spoke, hardly looked at each other. Hardly knew our names. Best I could tell at the time she was just being Tilda."

Our names.

In it together. Like a team.

"But, surely—surely she might have said something, or acted like—"

His face shrugs. *Nothing further to declare*, warns his face. He looks at the clock.

"Can we perhaps go into this more when we're not about to give dinner to hundreds of people?"

I exhale. "Of course." Check the clock, though my vision feels granular. How can he just leave it there? How can I?

Maybe he still doesn't understand it, himself. Or doesn't want to.

"Time to get cleaned up," he says.

"Yeah."

Both of us slowly standing, blinking at each other. We'll have to shake this off before the doorbell rings.

The oven clicks soothingly. Smells of lamb, potatoes, oil, garlic.

I reach up, draw down his stymied face, kiss his mouth, chin, cheeks. "You're next in the bathroom after me, laddie."

He affects a pout. "But I've done nothing *wrong*."

"And no swills, please," I add, able to breathe better. "A real shower. And please change your clothes. And underwear."

He flaps air from his lips, horse-like. "Right, Mummy."

I have only a few minutes to think it all over, under the stream of hot water.

The usual crowd, the usual revel. Snatching at olives, cheese, slices of bruschetta Neil has just pulled from the oven, when I hear Mike's *HA* through the screen door.

He's kept his laugh. It just takes longer to get out. Delayed, as if it has farther to travel. But his.

People drape the house, talking. Various rooms, backyard, a half-dozen of us messy-fingered around the starters in the kitchen. That's always my favorite part, the beginning, washing back the salt of olives and cheese with pulls of freezing beer. Gabbling, the beer taking hold fast. That's when I feel invincible and reckless, almost exquisitely alert. It may be argued that alcohol lends temporary powers, or at least injects us with that illusion: everyone in sight, no matter how grim my view of them by day, becomes almost stunningly dear. Heroic for showing up.

A jury of peers, laughing. Django on the music player, noise mounting. But nothing can camouflage Mike's thunder-crack.

Neil hears it too. We pause, glance at each other. Neil nods toward the oven: he's got to catch its next load. I drop my oily bruschetta, lick my fingers, scamper to the door.

Tilda has beat me. Her sturdy, square form blocks the light of dusk, propping the screen door open as Mike drags himself toward it, using a four-pronged walker cane. He's already made it up the porch stairs.

"Hi, Tilda. Welcome."

I lean to buss her cheek: criss-crossed with lines, moist, smelling of Dial soap. They must both have scrubbed down for the occasion.

I glance past them, the empty street, the yard. Electric blue, early stars. My chest automatically begins to rise, fill itself with new air—faintly honeysuckle, orange blossom. A mockingbird cached somewhere tries its best imitations, one after the next: first a chickadee, *chee-chee kew*, then a screeching jay, then a whip-poorwill; finally resorting, as if desperate, to the peeps of a fuzzy Easter chick. I can't see the bird itself, but want to applaud.

"Hullo, Rae." Tilda's voice comes low, dripping. Tilda is the only human I know who can make of the single word *hello* a lushly textured accusation. As if to remind you she certainly did indeed spot you that morning heaving a bloody corpse into the trunk of your car. Any response digs you deeper. Why? Who knows why? *La-la-la*, says her voice: *this is the way we get through it all.*

The only Tilda I've known.

I know what is coming, know what my role will be any evening Tilda visits. I will stand at the kitchen sink after dinner, washing and washing. Tilda will come stand beside me—none of the others singled out for this privilege, only me—arms folded, eyes shut. Talking. Talking. I will try not to inhale her body smell, her breath sour, sometimes actually fecal while she tells me about the perfection of Addie and Chet and prince Harry. Their villa, their furniture, the cactus garden, vacations in Cabo, Belize. Their best sound system. Best kitchen. Best best best. The barbecued spareribs and mashed potatoes she made last time she and Mike visited Albuquerque. (Yes, she wheeled him onto an airplane, shoehorned him in and out, round trip.) Expertise, from Tilda's mouth, is an overarching constant, an earth-sized parachute unfurled over everything. Her mastery in the tasting room; the devoted friendships with the winery people, restaurant employees, all in her path. To listen you'd presume her a society page doyenne, a food-and-wine Noel Coward. Pick any subject: Tilda will have nailed it, triumphed at it. Never mind she closes her eyes while telling you this, as if reading a script on the underside of her eyelids; never mind she smells bad and looks like she's slept on the sidewalk.

One thing never, ever gets mentioned.

Fish.

Aquaria.

Neil has made me swear on our marriage I won't broach it. Not one syllable. It's the deal I had to cut to get him to tell me the Spenders' story. Though it strikes me as the grossest denial, I've promised.

So I'll nod along as I wash. Make the noises. "No kidding. Really. Wow." Required words. Oil for the gears. And on she'll talk, and on.

A case study. Pathology. I should marshal my compassion, feel sad, sorry: There but for fortune. But the monologue grinds me down. And it's always me she goes after, me she isolates. Everyone else can relax into rhythms of normal conversation: observation, response. With Tilda it's strictly one way. Some kind of vendetta, is all I can think. I used to suppose she wanted to impress me. Later, I decided, it was a deliberate punishment. Zeroing in on me—so I imagine—because she senses I particularly loathe it, because somehow she knows it vexes me, drains me, more than it would anyone else. I hold my breath and stare at her greasy eyelids and think, *How can you not be aware of how you sound, how you look, what you are doing?*

No curiosity from her about my own existence. If I write books, if I cure cancer, it matters less than if I knit beer-can hats.

Mike has paused, leans patiently on his walker, waiting for his kiss. The only Mike I've known. Big Humpty Dumpty. Bald egg head, sunburn-red—the color gives him, paradoxically, a thriving air. Sheened with sweat from his effort to get through the door. Aloha shirt, jogging pants, thick socks, tennis shoes. It occurs to me suddenly, Tilda would have dressed him. Today, and every day. Who else? Under the jogging pants, a brace wraps the joints of his bad leg. His big body the kind we associate with the incapacitated: sloped shoulders, buttocks wide. The afflicted arm curls against his middle in an embryonic way, folded down at the wrist, the unused hand slender, slightly withered, soft as a woman's. He takes another step, first with the good leg; then hauls the other in its foam brace by angling his torso forward, pressing with the good arm on the cane for leverage, dragging the inert rest of himself. He grunts. Each step takes long, long minutes. A month ago Neil drove Mike to Candlestick Park to see a 49ers game, escorted him up and down those zillion concrete steps. It took me some exposure to Mike to appreciate what that must have involved. When I first met him I found the ordeal nearly unbearable; later I tried to invent ways to ease it, babbling small talk while he labored along to make it seem as if it didn't bother me. I still can't arrive at a way to behave during this ritual that isn't self-conscious, and I can never not be aware of it.

"Heya, Mikey! How's every scallawag thing?" I throw an arm around his neck, kiss the damp cheek. It too smells of Dial soap, and faintly, mildew.

He absorbs my embrace with concentration, the same way he concentrates on food. As if in prayer. As if to stop time. He fixes me with big dog eyes.

"Hul-lo . . . beauti- . . . beau-ti-ful . . . la-dy." The words come as slowly as his walk, the mouth groping, fierce to capture and utter each elusive syllable, plumbing it forth with supreme effort: his voice grainy and loud, so loud that people turn to stare. The smile is winsome, long-lashed, sweet as a baby's. Mike still flirts, partly in mischief, I think, mocking the hopelessness of his own predicament—a small self-amusement—and partly in earnest, an unkillable instinct.

But his eyes are lit with grief.

I have asked myself a million times how it must feel to be trapped inside the betraying body—numb, trussed, forced in shameful ways to be viewed and treated as a baby, or a dog. Everyone's forgotten a name or a word—just at the brink of speaking or writing it when it slips softly, hopelessly away, a coin into the ocean. Imagine that state as the constant: the gagged and muffled panic, answered only by blank ether.

"Ah, Mikey. If only." I shake my head, a secret part of me pleased by his admiration, the other parts peeved. I've scolded myself many times that Mike's admiration requires little more than owning a vagina. Also, flirting always distances you from whatever is really going on. I encourage it, for want of a better idea. But it's more than I can bear to look too long into those eyes.

"He thinks you're a goddess," Tilda says.

I glance quickly at her. Her eyelids are half-closed.

The blue air chills my ears.

To Mike she says calmly, "Let's get it rolling here now, shall we, buddy? We'll miss the meal at this rate."

⚜

THE HOUSE is overheated, steamy with bodies, clusters of people shouting at each other in every room, in the hall, even the bathroom, laughing too loudly (overriding the jazz); many open bottles grouped like small glass cities, food almost on—when the doorbell rings. When I throw it open, there is Addie.

The New Mexico goddess, before me on our front porch. Even through the smeary screen door, here it all is: the fabled beauty, the height, the figure—the sort of body that, eons ago, advertised Dior gowns. I feel reptilian. It pains me to recognize: Though I was no beauty, once I made that effect, or something like it—as a much younger woman, seeing older women's faces reconfigure an instant in an effort to camouflage haplessness, and on the heels of that—most difficult to acknowledge now—a seeping sadness. The memory places cool fingertips to my pulse.

"Addie! No one told us you were in town."

She laughs prettily, pleased at my amazement; blonde hair throwing a stripe of porchlight. She's wearing dark jeans, a lavender polo shirt, silver belt. Low buffed-silver heels, graceful silver earrings like delicate wings. She could be a commercial for clothing or shampoo, or face cream—

"Just flew in for a day or so," she says, and begins to explain the reason for her visit, shopping errands, to which I pay no attention because I am still so struck by her.

"Sorry I can't stay for dinner," she adds, and her clear, natural voice and movements signal at once that this is someone thoroughly practiced in every grace, every unuttered rule of making one's way at certain levels—knowledge I never had remotest truck with. Themed benefit galas; ice sculptures, champagne fountains. All the right language, the tones, quietly aware of her impact. But at least, no malevolence. No predation.

"Just wanted to stop by and say hi."

"Please! Please, come in. Would you like a glass of wine?"

She steps inside, a bewitching fragrance trailing her that I cannot immediately place. And the seas, of course, part for her. Neil spots her from the kitchen doorway and leaps toward her; at the same time, so does Tilda. Though Mike's planted on the couch and won't be able to get up without help, his damp red face shines as though someone had plugged it in. In the fuss that ensues, I'm able to study Addie's face. Honey-colored. Nose feminine, yet defined. Eyes like Mike's, big and deep, brown so dark you can't distinguish pupil from iris. Of course, Addie's eyes don't bear Mike's sorrowful light. Her gaze is attuned, calm, steady. It occurs to me she could have piloted aircraft. Addie moves first to hug and kiss her father; then to Tilda and Neil, then trades handshakes all round (a thin diamond bracelet sparkling back and forth over the slender wrist). Well-wishers crowd in. Neil and Tilda and I stand back while the usual questions are put: how she likes it in the Southwest, what about the food, how little Harry fares. Albuquerque suits her well; food's better than you'd imagine, Harry's doing wonderfully, thanks. Her banter is easy, capable—not especially forthcoming or original—but equable. She likes her life. She has no plans to give it away.

Tilda stands apart, smiling. That's when it comes to me: She will be extra-obnoxious beside me at dish duty tonight. Now that I've seen the miracle product for myself, close up. She'll expect my awe.

Lord, what an unkind thought.

I take Addie's hand when she bids us goodbye. It's impossible not to like her.

"Hey Mikey, look at this. Remember Vache Qui Rit?" I brandish a silver-foiled wedge.

He is seated in his original position on the couch, plate in his lap. He chews slowly, seriously, as he always does, concentrating. Food is one of Mike's last joys. (Neil and I have never broached the sex question—whether Mike still experiences it and if so, how. I'm positive neither of us wants to think about it—though if I let the thought in, I can guess. I'm sorry; it makes me a little sick.) Tilda sits beside the great lump of him, positioning his napkin in the top of his sweatshirt, cutting up his food. He can chew and swallow and taste. He can wield a fork.

The living room windows make square black patches, reflecting lamplight. Neil hunches in his leather chair, forking up meat and potatoes. His eating style has always rankled me, though I do my utmost to ignore it: the British thing of never putting a utensil down, working a little pile of food onto the back of the fork, popping it in, repeating till everything's gone. Methodic, silent, fast as a wolf. Fixated, as if someone held a stopwatch over him, poised to rip the plate from him. When I protest he shrugs, changes the subject. His plate used to be fair game, I know. His father, a welder, would grab whatever Neil had not crammed down in the space of the minutes it took the father to cram down his own food. No matter this hasn't been true for over forty years, no matter it's the twenty-first century and people routinely engage in a practice, known for its relaxing properties, called dinner conversation: Neil's programmed, and no hint I drop, no frank hand pressing an arm or kick under the dining table can ever seem to get him to put the fork down now and again and *say something for God's sake*.

So I say the something.

Maybe it's just how quiet things get when people start eating. Maybe it's the two beers I've drunk—gone down so quickly between bites of food, producing that instant floating relief, the fondness, the bravura. It doesn't seem so radical to lift the little silver wedge from the tray on the coffee table, turn it in my fingers so it flashes lamplight like a platinum doubloon.

"Remember, Mikey?"

Light the color of whiskey frames the faces around the room. Voices in the kitchen, behind them the vibraphone of Milt Jackson, "Nature Boy," tones that shiver and melt in the air, an aural borealis.

There was a boy, a very strange enchanted boy.

Mike looks at the flashing silver wedge in my hand, still chewing. He stares at it. Tilda takes a bite of food, blasé. Neil looks up, chewing, as the silence lengthens. After a while, so do the others.

Mike's brown eyes have welled red as he chews and swallows. His nostrils twitch and redden, and big oily tears crest the berms of flesh beneath his eyes, spilling down his sunburnt cheeks.

"What in Christ's name did you want to go do that for?" Neil is slamming things into containers while I wash.

"You're the one who brought the fucking cheese home in the first place," I hiss, though my stomach hurts. It is the worst thing on earth to fight on a full stomach.

He moves around grabbing things. "But what were you thinking?"

"C'mon, sweetheart. Don't do this. Didn't Tilda remind us? He cries easily. Drop of a hat. That's how stroke victims express emotions; they're at the surface all the time. He cried at my reading, too, remember?"

In fact, I wish I could lose the memory: Rows of people packed in close, smiling at me under white store lights, holding their cookies, their cups of herb tea. The Book Stash had long ago ceded to marketing trends, sold its square footage to a local franchise called Messersmiths, the only independent in Mira Flores that still keeps nostrils above the flood line of superstores. I'd phoned or scribbled cards to friends urging them to come, to bring anyone upright and breathing. At readings I tend to disappear into the feel of the voice in my throat, the willful music composing itself on the fly, secret messages working themselves out in the sounds: unforeseen, cryptic messages; the words themselves almost pointless, for some reason only sound mattering. I'd just finished reading a chapter from "Comet Camp," I think it was—a tender passage, at least to me. Writers sniff that it's stale to compare books to offspring, but I feel that way. It still makes me happy to be friends with them—the books, I mean.

I'd pronounced the final line, my eyes sweeping the faces before me, pausing to light for an instant on this one or that, wondering for a beat what the owner of the face might be thinking, then moving to the next—a sideways pan so practiced I hardly think about it anymore. And at the back of the smiling rows shone Mike's big red egg-head, his red face streaming tears. Tilda sat beside him, nonchalant.

Oh, fuck, was my first thought. *I've messed with him somehow. Traumatized him.*

But how? The passages I'd read had not, I reminded myself, been sad. When I caught Tilda at the door to thank her for coming, Mike was a few paces beyond us in his wheelchair. I asked her quietly what his tears meant. Tilda shrugged, cheerful in her smirking, contemptuous way. By then I had internalized the facts: she despised everything I stood for, but Mike loved me like a dog. We would cooperate in a pantomime of friendship for Mike's sake.

Neil hadn't been at the bookstore that night—I've asked him not to attend readings; his appraising gaze, serious and penetrating, makes me self-conscious. I'd described Mike's tears to him afterward at home, and Tilda's offhand explanation.

"Remember when I told you about it?"

Pulling on my yellow rubber gloves, stirring soapsuds with the scrubber.

Neil spoons leftovers into plastic cartons, spilling some onto the wooden island, his features working.

"What've you got against him, anyway?"

I turn from the soapy dishes to face him.

"For God's sake, give it a rest, Neil! I've got nothing against Mike anymore. I just feel sorry as hell for the guy."

He looks at me, piling containers into the crook of his arm.

"I don't believe that."

"What can I do to convince you?" The ache in my belly congeals.

Neil bangs plates as he stacks them, silverware clattering off onto the table.

"You've always hated him. You try to cover it but I can see it. Because he was a womanizer. You think he was influencing me to do the same."

This is not exactly false, but neither is it that simple. I move to gather the silver Neil has left, plopping them into the empty sink: they ring out against the enamel.

"That's not completely true, Neil. I did hate that Mike was a hound dog, at first. I did worry he might persuade you to—to be like that, to imitate him. But that was back at the beginning. Now I'm just sorry for the poor guy. He was part of a generation that did that stuff all the time—I know that, Neil. I'm sorry as hell he's paralyzed. And I'm sorriest of all for him because of Tilda."

Not the best tactic, but I've seized on it in a burst of defensive righteousness. Neil's scowl deepens.

"And what of her? What is it with you and Tilda?"

I try to take a breath, but my chest feels constricted, fist-size.

"Sweetheart, even you have to admit Tilda is not the easiest person to be with. She hates me. I swear it. Yet for some reason she gets in my face—sort of a punishment. Or that's how it feels. I can't figure it out. Every dinner party I'm the one standing here by the sink listening to her—nobody else, Neilly, not even you; it's always me she goes for—wedges right in, practically on top of me, bragging. The whole night. I can't get a word in. Inches from me, and her breath is horrible—I'm sorry but it's like shit, her breath, the kind of breath that tells you a person's not taking care of herself. All the time she talks I try to respond—and she seems to hate me more the nicer I try to be. Even you felt it once—you told me so, remember?"

This isn't strictly true either. He'd said he glimpsed her hatred, but sensed it wasn't exactly directed toward him.

He steps past me to take the sponge; begins wiping down the island's wooden countertop. His big hand whisks along.

"In the lost childhood of Judah, Christ was betrayed," he murmurs.

"*What* did you say?"

"I said, is it possible for you to consider she might feel jealous," he says quietly.

"But jealous of what?"

He looks at me evenly.

"Think about it."

I gape at him. Of course he's right. My husband is whole. Sentient. I don't have to bathe, feed, dress him, help him shit, wait eternities for him to stand or sit or speak, tense myself to catch and right him as he hauls the inert half of himself across a room or up a few steps. I'm not the default breadwinner, carry no responsibility for a permanent 200-pound infant who requires round-the-clock medicines, hydrotherapy, driving—God knows what else—alongside my own full-time job, laundry, groceries, cooking, cleaning. Paperwork. Bills.

"I see her managing a thankless task," Neil says, as if summarizing my thoughts.

"Close to heroic," he adds.

His voice is hard, his eyes set, their lovely caramel centers cold and oblique. I hate his face this way; it frightens me. It's as if the Neil I know has died and some robotic device has taken up residence in him. Our ease, our jokes, my kissing his warm neck, its clean custardy scent, the catch of light in his eyes—gone. But worst, it feels as though his *memory* of our sweetness together, his desire for it, valuing of it, have vanished as well.

"Why can't you let it be what it is," he says. "Has everybody got to have a Nobel Prize before you'll speak to them?"

He has turned from me, leans his forehead against the back door, its window glass yielding nothing but his own reflection. It's completely dark outside.

"Not many folks are gon'ta fit inside that pure little white envelope, where you admit the worthy," he said. *Werrrr*thy, is how it sounded.

"I don't know what lot you think you're savin' it up for," he says. "But I've a strong hunch no one's gonna pass muster. No one'll ever be good enough. Includin' me," he adds.

I can't think how to answer. My stomach dropped and twisting.

"Why can't you just let it *be*," he says again, still turned from me.

All the arguments I've mulled, that Neil refuses to hear—*Not one word*, he has warned me—arguments that surely, surely Tilda Krall created the nightmare that befell her; that as concretely as I stand here Tilda was the marauder in galoshes with a base-ball bat who loosed all her rage on what her husband most loved, who brought on his stroke, his mauled, crippled life, and (wittingly or not) her own imprisonment in that life—those arguments never find voice. If Neil—rational, systematic, sane Neil—secretly believes it to be true, he will never, ever say so. And will never, so long as we are together, allow it to be said.

Loyalty? Or that sturdy British reflex for covering over?

Either way. Our me-and-you conspiracy, the tender code between us—I'll do anything to get them back.

My love.

The couples man.

"Neil, for heaven's sake. Look at me."

Soon after that night, Tilda decamps. Moves herself and Mike to Albuquerque.

She sends a note in the mail with their new address, a scribbled few lines. She wants to be near the kids, near little Harry. It is warm in summer there, and for winters, well, Tilda writes, they'll just have to "hunker down and run up the heating bill."

She has found a ground floor condominium, wheelchair access, carport. (Stairs, alas, lead to the bedrooms and main bath, but Mike needs to practice his stairs, and if in time he cannot manage them he can sleep in the living room.) She has taken a job with the deli and wine section of an upscale gourmet market. Her managers are angels from heaven, giving her flexible hours once they grasp the situation with Mike.

They also give her, miraculously, basic medical insurance. Her social security, and some of her prior coverage, carry over. Chet and Addie will of course subsidize everything.

A few weeks after the card arrives Tilda phones, asking us to visit. "Mike misses you guys most of all," she says. Because she is talking to Neil when she says it, I am spared guessing how much of her tone may be irony-free.

Neil says he'll get right back to her. Replaces the receiver. Looks at me.

"I can go by myself, Rae, if you'd rather—"

"I'll bring books," I interrupt, meeting his eyes.

Neil's brows begin to beetle.

"No, dummy," I tell him. "Not my own! Something funny. I know one that will make him laugh himself—" I am about to say *sick*.

The Bear Went Over the Mountain. Kotzwinkle. The apartment will shake with Mike's crazy barks. Mike is actually very like that bear character, galumphing, smelly, lash-battingly sincere. Irresistible to women. Maybe the similarity will enwrap his awareness in a comforting way.

I'll take a few days' leave from the office. It won't kill them to scavenge a sub for that long.

"—It'll make him laugh himself silly," I finish, with what I hope passes for aplomb.

Neil's face relaxes. I snug up to him, backwards.

"Squeeze my shoulders?"

*M*uch to be said for high desert, especially mornings, especially summer. Best of my Arizona memories but cooler, cleaner. Sky the bruised white of doves, gashed with yellow. Birdsong unfamiliar, exuberant, liquid. Scent of creosote, like new rain— a smell I remember adoring—and mesquite, peppery cactus blossom. Breathing in in in just to keep tasting it, line the inside of your lungs, never stop inhaling.

Lemon-colored weed flowers like tiny upside-down skirts. Beyond, hills of brownish lavender dotted with scrub.

This, from the opened patio door. A palm is out here too, dusty, chest-high, fatly thriving from a hole cut for it in the concrete, or rather the concrete poured round it, pleated fans for leaves, translucent edges flickering in currents of air. I stand with my coffee, breathing. Sky phases from powder to ghost of robin's egg. And that scent, clean as snow. In in in. Maybe I could return to my roots, at a higher altitude.

"Neilly, I love this place."

I turn to call it into the kitchen where Neil is parked on a stool at the counter, Lincoln legs planting his feet on the floor. Tilda is busy frying up the kind of breakfast I have taught him over years, armed with horrifying statistics, to forego: sausage, eggs, bacon, bagels, butter, preserves, cream cheese, smoked salmon. A box of chocolate truffles sits open on the counter. (Surgeons must saw through the sternum, I've explained to him more than once, to gain access to the heart. A special electric saw. Imagine the *sound*, I urge him. Neil shakes his head against it, like a horse.) Tilda wears a black sweatshirt bearing a Grateful Dead skull and cross-bones, baggy jeans, barefoot. She hums, moving about. Tumblers full of milky-pink gin fizz stand before Neil, Mike's place setting, mine. Tilda's glass is pinkly empty, but I know she is draining, by quiet turns, the leftovers from the blender; and when those are done, commencing on a half-empty champagne bottle left from last night.

A coffee-shop smell snakes from the opened sliding-glass door into virgin air.

"Neil, the desert is heavenly. Reminds me of my childhood. Can we live here?"

Laughter in the kitchen.

"Location slut," Neil says, smiling at his newspaper.

Tilda calls, "Mike would love it." She ladles a mound of shiny scrambled eggs onto Neil's plate. Satellite jazz radio, Louis Armstrong and Ella Fitzgerald, *Autumn in New York*. Our gifts are piled on the side table, *The Bear Went Over the Mountain* on top. Newspapers litter the sofa. Neil's made space by his plate for the page of legal announcements he's studying.

He looks up to grin at me through the opened sliding glass. "Let's pick up a real estate brochure today. Just to see."

More laughter. "We have a plan!"

Neil is so happy to be near Mike again, to be away from work, to confront the ready bonus of forbidden foods and liquor, he's beaming from all parts of himself. I'd forgotten how much he likes to get away. In the upstairs guest bed last night (posters of benign desertscapes on the wall, like a motel) he imitated Bogart, tilting my chin up, squinting, curling his upper lip. Intensifies the burr so the line grows funnier still. "Of ahll the gin joints in ahll the toownes in ahll the werrld, she walks inta maene."

I've underestimated how much he misses Mike. Seeing them hunched side by side on the couch watching football reruns, yelling at the screen, stuffing themselves with beer and chips, salsa and hummus and cheese and pickles and clam dip. They could be Addams Family characters: spectral carrot-top—though in recent years he's acquired a wee belly, size of a small throw pillow—seated beside Humpty Dumpty. Neil's frenzied commentary, three beats of silence, Mike's wall-cracking bark.

"Go go go go c'mon c'mon c'mon—"

"———HAH!"

"NO, idiot! Och, ye had time! All the time in the werrld! Bloody wanker!"

"———HAH!"

For a moment you'd think, judging with eyes half-closed, we were a wholesome club. Two middle-aged, middle class couples, wisecracking, everything in common. Getaway weekend. History blurs—astonishingly—to dim, distant shapes, a dream someone had. That Mike happens to be incapacitated seems the most minor of facts, transposed now to this tranquil university neighborhood. The prior life? The glad-handing ombudsman, self-appointed king of marine life—the nightmare of destruction, striking down the handsome giant, rendering him into a wet-eyed, garbled substance—if not erased then scarcely remembered and in any case, unnecessary. Whatever happened no longer matters. It occurs to me, watching the shop fronts out the car window, that this ease of forgetting underlies all our conditions, all our aging, irrespective of trauma. Things move on. People move on. One's story's not wanted. We park along the ample streets, load Mike from car into wheelchair and back. Sun bathes us, yellow weed blossoms poking through the curb. Passersby glance at us and look elsewhere, complacent, respectful. Everyone doing their part. The city flows on like any hundred others.

Tilda drove us around yesterday in similar weather, narrating. The sky matched the O'Keeffe painting: platoons of white puffs marching across a field of bright, depthless blue. We cruised Memorial Hospital, where Harry was born. We stopped at Oppenheimer, the high-end market where Tilda works—she calls it Opulent-heimer—met the managers amid shelves of gleaming wine bottles, bins filled with Italian cheeses, salamis, jars of bright peppers and olives. In their dark green aprons the managers joked, clapped us on the back. We saw the fancy golf course and abutting it, through a private iron gate opened by electric keypad, Chet and Addie's villa. A paved drive wound us past stands of palo verde, cactus, raked gravel, and then there it was. Pueblo-style, sprawling. Stucco outside, interior blond, sleek Danish wood. Oak floors shining like a decor magazine's. Here at last the famous cactus garden, white quartz rocks veined with glitter. Four bathrooms. No one home but a cleaning lady, a shrunken, ageless woman, black hair pulled tight in a knot from which spilled a skein so long it reached nearly to the backs of her knees. Thinner than a child in sweatshirt and jeans; body a stick-puppet's, hung from a skull-like head. She was standing on a stepladder with a cloth and spray bottles, cleaning the top surfaces of the highest linen cupboards—also of oak—surfaces no one would ever touch, or see. "*Hóla*, Esperanza," Tilda called. Esperanza stopped and turned to face us on her perch, standing to attention as if for military review. Someone had told her this was how she must greet her employers. When she smiled her face crinkled everywhere in a kind of weary helpless sweetness, so tightly over her bones I thought her face might shred. She can't weigh seventy-five pounds, I thought, as she and Tilda went through their *como estas, nuestros amigos, que bueno*. In the course of it Mike managed to locate and haul up and shout the word *Hóla*! at her, collapsing afterward into a relieved grin.

"Seven kids," Tilda whispered after we'd passed, pushing Mike along. "Husband bigger than King Kong."

"She looks exhausted," I murmured.

"Wouldn't you?" Tilda shot back.

Right, I thought, feeling my chest tighten. Tilda owns the knowledge, as usual. I said nothing. But what gave Tilda her snitty presumptiveness, this casual, smug dominion?

Neil said quietly, "Her life is probably better here than it would be in Mexico, though I know that is not a happy reality." He didn't turn around as he spoke, or address the remark to any single one of us, but kept walking. Mike, lulled by the rolling motion of his chair, half-dozed as Tilda wheeled him. Our voices echoed in the blond corridors, cool and gleaming, our sandals clacking. Little Harry was off at his Montessori school, Chet and

Addie working. It must take them weeks, I thought, to *find* each other around here.

Today we will head for an oyster bar. It serves martinis, we've been advised, in which little goldfish loll, carved of raw ginger. Never mind the breakfast before us: the oyster bar's the goal. Never mind what may or may not be good for Mike. Mike wants martinis and raw oysters on the half shell. Cigars for afterward, to my horror. Neil has brought two expensive Cubans, God knows from where, smuggled in a plastic bag in his toilet kit.

Staring at the mounds of fatty breakfast, it's suddenly clear to me—though why it has not struck me sooner I'm unable to say—we've been inducted, pledged to the sort of drama you read about: bringing scotch to the cirrhosis victim, cigarettes to the doomed sod breathing through a hole in his throat. Tilda has deputized us to assist. Offerings to the great eminence because he has begged it, because he implores and demands it, after doctors have assured him these very indulgences will finish him off.

Our great eminence has dwelt overlong this morning in the downstairs bathroom, mere paces from the kitchen counter. For faster access to him, Tilda has strung a curtain across the doorway in lieu of a door. She rattles away at the stove, unconcerned. Platters manifest: fried meats, more eggs, toast. A round of brie has appeared. I've offered to help, been waved off. But now I'm summoned: fresh fruit to peel and cut. The fruit is, I know, a concession. "Rae's a health nut," Neil told her at last night's dinner (a pile of bloody steaks) as I kicked him under the table. There it smolders now on my forehead, the scarlet brand. Still, I'm secretly elated for fresh apples, oranges, bananas, grapes, strawberries. Something clean to eat and also to fool with, a bit of business. Standing beside Neil and his newspaper, I set to work. The orange peel spritzes oily mist as I thumb it from its clasp.

We can hear Mike now, grunting through the curtain. My heart drops. He is on the toilet, struggling to move his bowels not fifteen feet from the breakfast table, behind a thin cloth so loosely strung that if you glance (I turn aside) you can easily see his yellowy nakedness, fore and aft. But looking away won't be enough: an aroma, powerful, confirms all suppositions. More grunts, moans—alarmingly, like those of sexual transport. He calls for help.

"Til-DA!"

We look at her. She turns off the kitchen tap, checks the stove burners, dries her hands at the sink.

"TIL-da!"

Hangs the dishtowel with care on the oven handle. Straightens her sweatshirt.

To Neil and me, pleasantly: "S'cuse."

The spreading stench. Mike's gasps.

"TIL-DA!"

I look at the hot food piled about, and think I may suddenly have to vomit. Without looking at Neil or at anyone, I jump up and flee outside, holding my breath.

True to the warnings and medical stats, in 2008 the second stroke hits. Three years have passed since the first.

The news reaches us by telephone at dinnertime Monday, end of the workday, mid-November. Chet has made the call; Neil answers. Mike has been taken to Memorial in Albuquerque, where Harry was born. Chet is calling from the waiting room.

We have just eaten; I'm in my socks, carrying the refilled water pitcher from the sink, using both hands so I don't strain a wrist.

Neil repeats the message to me without inflection, after hanging up.

"Oh, Neilly," I say, setting the pitcher on the counter. "Oh, sweetheart."

He says nothing more, but sits and glowers into air a moment. It occurs to me he's been checkmated again, this time in an irreducible way. This is where men's power ends; the medical pronouncement, the hospital bedside. At length he jumps up, grabs his car keys and stalks out, letting the screen door slam. I don't yell after him or try to catch him. I'll let him have his anguish whole this time, let him stew without my Good Ship Lollipop suggestions enraging him further. His car engine revs, backs out of the driveway. Then the evening resumes its stillness. A weeknight, work night, the city tucked tightly down until the weekend's liberation. Clocks set back now, dark so early. I stare at the bulb light in the refrigerator, imagining the same light in the hospital room, Tilda center stage. Addie and Chet will have instantly arrived. I picture all of them huddled together, talking with doctors, administrators, each other. Wonder how long they've been there, who they'll have found to look after Harry—or maybe Harry's there, too. Maybe they'll have brought the toddler as a form of treatment, to coax Mike back.

Back from what?

I go to the bedroom, shuck my work clothes and underwear. Relief to slip on the worn t-shirt, flannel bottoms; cottony, no bindings, breasts free, ah. Men's genitals must feel that way loosed from their underwear; must be why men always handle themselves once their genitals are freed. Except men love any chance to handle themselves. I am thinking this as I finish the dishes, put on water for tea, pad around closing window-shades in the half-dark house, open the refrigerator again, the cupboard doors, yearning for chocolate. Take out the cereal, put the cereal back. Slice a Fuji apple. Walk from room to room, chewing. The water boils. Chamomile, smell of fresh hay. Back into the darkened living room, carrying my steaming cup. Sit. Get up at once, motor to the kitchen, fill a bowl with cereal, pour chocolate syrup over it, milk. Bear it like an Egyptian offering to the living room. Find the remote, flick through channels, give each a half-second before clicking past. In that half-second I can generate a half-dozen synopses for whatever idiocy is being pitched. I can write the entire script of a series from that glimpsed half-second: who will die, marry, betray. Part of me thinks this admirable and clever. The other part feels as shamed as if Jesus Christ had marched in and heaved the television monitor through the window. But when you need to leave your own head, stupid television can help. It can make hours go by, dozens of moron channels at a time.

I settle for ballroom dancing. Men and women, Los Angeles tans, feathers and satin and lamé: entwined like cobras, heads reared back, eyes locked, gliding around. The women's smiles look maddened, flames lick their eyes. Teeth bleached so white you have to blink. Clenched faces lean back beholding each other, whirling around, murderous. Still, the dancing hypnotizes me. Perfect synchrony. The women's gowns trail after the moving couples like smears of icing, lemon, crimson, popsicle blue. Fox trot, tango, waltz. I set down the cereal bowl, lengthen my spine, sit forward. I love to dance. Neil doesn't. If he's very drunk he'll stand opposite me with a sweet, sheepish expression, doing a kind of Frankenstein two-step, but maybe we—maybe I could convince him—

I hear the car roar into its dock. Slam of door, slam of trunk, rattling bags. Neil pushes the front door open with a foot, bearing two stuffed grocery bags. He advances into the kitchen, dumps the bags, passes me peeling off his jacket.

"Odds aren't good, you know," he mutters.

I sit up, punch off the dancers.

"I know that, sweetheart. I remember."

Tilda had warned us in Albuquerque. Statistics were lousy. Strokes tend to revisit, often fatally. It was the reason she and Mike had blown all his late mother's money; the reason she gave him steaks and oysters and martinis and cigars.

I sit in the dark. Until now it has never occurred to me we might actually lose Mike. I kept the logic pushed offstage. One finds endless ways to repress it. In my reasoning (though reason is surely not what this is), Mike led a prior life as a muscleman, then as the local Mr. Wizard, the downtown dime-store scientist, handing out gimcracks, shouting, joking with passersby. But those were years before my time here, and as it now stands (the non-reasoning goes) Mike will always be around in his present form, a big dense doe-eyed pile of ectoplasm, and we'll all just carry on in our little constellation of wine-soaked dinners for as long as anyone can imagine. That's how it has been, how it must continue to be. Crippled, exasperating, cartoonish Mike, Neil's oldest American friend, the slow gentle child who laughs too loudly too late, who craves affection like a dog and flirts like a halfwit and suffers, behind closed doors, like Prometheus.

The way of things.

Neil strides to the bathroom. I hear the toilet seat bang up, the patient stream of urine (oh finite, faithful body!), the brief silence while he gives it its shake, the flush, sink water running.

I hear his steps enter the kitchen: liquor cupboard door mewing open. Clink of bottle against bottle, whish of freezer door swung wide, freezer air blowing, ice skittering over the cutting board as it's popped from the tray. Blub-blubbing of liquid over ice.

Bags crackle as they empty. Objects thunk down.

I push myself up, pad into the kitchen. Neil is intent, sawing the plastic wrap from an enormous raw turkey. Arrayed about him like amphitheater tools: packets of gravy mix, stuffing, cans of cranberry sauce, canister of salt, peppercorns, baster, ladle, chopping knife, carrots, onions, celery, colander, several of the biggest plastic bowls we own. Well out of range of harm stands his tumbler of Glenlivet, two rocks. Neil's going to stuff and bake a turkey. Tomorrow before work he will strip the bird and put the carcass and bones in his biggest pot to simmer, for stock.

Turkeys are on sale, very inexpensive just now. We have two others in the freezer.

"Not good," he repeats, looking up at me.

*L*ike an afterthought it happens, in a breath. Tilda and Addie are standing by his bed during a routine visit in late November, when Mike goes.

The nurse is bathing him. A regular morning, elevenish. Sun through the window, orderlies and nurses and interns striding past the open door pushing gurneys, loudspeaker paging Doctor Mukterjee, silver stethoscopes and dangling identification tags flashing against scrubs, scents of heavily creamed coffee and disinfectant, elevator doors chiming down the hall. A routine function, the bathing. Tilda and Addie are standing to the side, languid eyes on the nurse's movements, chatting about where they might go pick up some lunch. The nurse, a big woman (she'd have to be), has gently turned Mike on his side to wipe down his back and torso. Her name is Charlotte, they find out later. Mike's skin where his clothes have covered it is pale yellow, like an old tusk.

He gives out a long sigh, and dies.

We've been waiting all week, knowing nothing.

We decide to phone Tilda that evening: the amount of time that has passed without news, following the second stroke, worries us to alarm. I poke my head into the living room to warn Neil, who sits unseeing in front of the television news hour.

"Neilly, I'm gonna phone her now."

He nods, not looking at me. The mouths open and close in the heads on the screen, men in suits, their faces gray-pink, cheeks spilling over their collars.

I go to the bedroom, pick up the phone, punch in the numbers for Tilda's home, expecting her to be at the hospital, expecting her machine's recording to click on. Tilda answers on the second ring.

This so startles me that the words I've prepared fly off like frightened birds.

"Tilda? It's Rae. We—were—concerned about Mike, and we just wanted—to—um, let you know we've—been thinking about him, thinking about you both and we're both—"

Neil appears in the bedroom doorway.

Tilda's voice interrupts. Serene, dreamy.

"Rae. Hello, Rae. How very interesting you should call right now. As a matter of fact Addie and I were just at the hospital this morning, and Mike died while he was being washed by the nurse."

She says this the way you'd say, *Why, I happened to buy some shoes exactly like yours this very morning.*

Later I remind myself she would have been heavily tranquilized.

"Oh, Tilda. Oh God."

I slap my hand over the mouthpiece and mouth it to Neil. His eyes go wide; his face crumples.

"Tilda," I say. "My God, I am so sorry, we are so—Tilda, was there—I mean, may I ask—"

"Just kind of let out a sigh while she was turning him on his side, and died," she says.

Lilting, breezy. Perfectly elocuted.

"Addie and Chet are here with me now," she adds.

Her voice lyrical, singsong. She is smashed. This time I bless the alcohol, the meds, both.

"Tilda, we are crushed; I cannot tell you how, how much, how terrible we—" and then Neil snatches the phone from my hand.

As he speaks into the receiver, to my amazement, my husband begins to sob.

"Tilda," Neil says, crying so hard he can scarcely get the words out. He pushes a fist against his forehead. Sags to the bed.

"Tilda, I'm so sorry," he says. His voice is broken. "So sorry. Is there anything we can do, Tilda. Anything at all."

Tilda must be making the *not-now-but-later-thank-you* noises on the other end of the phone; Neil listens and weeps. He keeps saying "Anything at all." I look on, dumbfounded. I have only seen Neil cry once before, when his father died. It was something he contained fast, like a small kitchen fire—not like this.

When he hangs up he slumps over, covering his face. In the yellow light of the bedside lamp I kneel before him, slip my arms around his back, press my cheek against his chest, nuzzle upward, kiss his neck, the soft place where it curves into shoulder, where he smells like custard and I like to warm my nose.

"Sweetheart. Sweetheart."

"Mike was—part—of—"

"I know, sweetheart. Part of your life. Your world."

But how can I know? By what right may I ever claim to know? The man who'd all but defined Neil's first years in this country. The friendship, the ocean rescue, the family, the steak dinners, the fucking drive-in movies. The bail-outs. The women, the cigars, the bravado. The rearing of the girl. The grandchild. The great fall, its wretched aftermath. Years of the childlike rendition of the man. What can it add up to?

Probably this is what most horrifies Neil. It adds up to nothing.

Addie is a delightful being, of course, and little Harry, naturally. But when you think of people, of the shape their lives take, your first instinct is not to measure them by their children.

By what, then? Not what newspapers write. Not what preachers or politicians recite.

Neil, like all of us, is alone with it.

Silent the winter night, the house.

After some minutes, he quiets. Raises his gaze, meeting mine straight on.

"I am not happy," he says.

And it is not grief, but me he accuses.

$\mathcal{T}$ilda and Addie have organized a party. Or that's not the right word. Gathering.

It is February, cold. Chet cannot attend, bound to finish the business's tax obligations in Albuquerque. Tilda has flown over, with Addie and Harry. They're holding the event in Mira Flores because most of Mike's original tribe dwells here: a chance, we guess, to let people say goodbye. Cocktail hour, late afternoon. They've staged it at the Hilton—Tilda and Addie have booked adjoining rooms—a name that by this time in the nation's life no longer evokes shining marble surfaces and crystal and perfume, and uniformed service people scurrying here to there clutching big vases of hothouse flowers or delivering telegrams on silver trays; but rather the bleak, Soviet, linoleum-and-cleaning-fluid surfaces of a leased franchise. It is run by a Pakistani who hires Mexicans to do all the grunt work. They look at us only an instant as they pass, tiredly, before looking away.

Neil and I have parked in the lot, turned off the engine, sit staring at the buildings. The hotel complex is stationed on a hill—air a bit fresher, views of the town below, vineyard hills beyond. A flat brownish rag of pollution floats above, in blue light. Whining over the freeway, fat and predatory, a helicopter. Radio traffic reporter? Cops hunting down a fugitive? Medevac? No one knows, and in the frantic crisscross of eternal cars, no one will find out. The city carries on, endlessly retracing its hamster-wheel patterns in Futuropolis haze. Terrible things happen on the highway, in the world; hunger riots, suicide bombers, oil spills, malignant moles. It's all the same: we have no room in our Day-Timers for more such news, so we've given up wanting to know.

⌘

OUR THERAPIST is Artie Schumann ("like the composer, the composer!"), an old New Yawka with a long white ponytail. Tells us we're fighting about amounts. Amounts can be modified, he says, poured back and forth till we get them right. Apothecary therapy. We see him Wednesday nights; afterward, for a reward, we go eat someplace. I make sure to shake Artie's hand when we rise to leave. There's always something infantilizing about facing off with a therapist. We both feel the sea change the moment we step in, the meekness, the shrinking; the ceiling floats higher and higher and the chairs grow bigger around us, our legs dangling. Everything that comes out of our mouths feels puny and wiggly as bacteria. When we finally stand to leave, I deliberately clasp Artie's hand and look him in the eye to re-establish us as intelligent adults—the gesture of the handshake never seems to have occurred to him, or maybe it's forbidden; body contact too dangerous to risk.

As soon as we're outside his door we look at each other: "Well?" Occasionally we're angry, yelling in the elevator. Other times we burst out laughing: Artie's so old he's gone a little nuts. Favors long anecdotes that may or may not have a point. Squints all the time, as if his shoes pinched. Says everything twice: "Do things! Do things!"—peering under stacks of files for papers he can't find; copies of aphorisms, quotations from weird sources, Winnie the Pooh, science fiction. He told us he grabs random books from the library shelves—hides their titles from his own gaze—to see what they'll disclose when he gets them home, what nuggets they'll feed him. Library I Ching. Urges us to go out more. Play more. Part of our homework, he says. Play as homework. I wonder whether going to memorial cocktail parties counts.

I am doing Artie's bidding, because I am frightened.

Somewhere along the years of my good-natured bitching, without my grasping it, Neil became bedrock. Our lives flow along the granite floor and boulder banks of his making. What am I, finally, without him? An aging typist with an unprofitable hobby. True, I've written books—four now, since we met. Two novels, two story collections, with little more effect than bowling trophies. (They do make handy presents. Except people are tongue-tied when they next see you because they haven't read your book and never intend to; or if they did read it they have quarrels with it, or they hate the cover, or the book has so confused or embarrassed or shocked and appalled them they're embarrassed to bring it up.)

Alone, what have I? Parents dead. No other relatives, at least that I know of. Two or three friends from long-ago single days. They live out of state, tend complicated families, send Christmas photos of kids. Neil never actually said, "I'm quitting if things don't change," but the night of Mike's death, his face said it. I wept all night beside him in the bed while he slept. Mascara marks on the pillow, after daylight came, looked like small paw prints. I wanted to puke, but puke wouldn't come. When he woke in the night to my sobs, he acted like someone observing a stranger who'd just broken her leg. "Yes," he noted mildly, drifting back to sleep. "It must be very painful."

In the morning he wanted to fuck, as usual. My burning eyes swollen nearly shut.

It took us time to find Artie. (We saw one man before him who sat nervous, mute. A traffic light would have given more direction. He stared at us bug-eyed when we used the word *ennui*.) Then one of the women at my office suggested Artie. (Women don't blanch about these matters. *Dry cleaner, library, gym, organic fruit, rescue marriage, face cream.*) Neil likes Artie, thank God. I think he enjoys Jewish types; the nasally, audacious pronouncements. Though I notice, once we're seated in that room padded with African carvings and Artie's bad paintings and musty books, Neil waits a long, long time to speak. This annoys me, but I say nothing about it. Instead I address both of them, Artie and Neil, my voice going shriller, dragging my eyes from one to the other as if they were a two-headed tribunal. Telling them I feel like a wishbone cracking: trying to cover my job, my writing, my wifely ministerings to a mysteriously unhappy man. I still can't make sense of why Neil objects to me *now*. I'm the same Rae I always was, doing the same Rae things—at least it feels that way. Last session, in a desperate spasm, I blurted to Artie what Neil had told me the night of Mike's death: *I don't know why I'm with you.* It felt thrilling to utter the words, like I'd flipped a slab of raw liver onto the center of the floor, glistening with droplets of dark blood against the beige carpet. Artie had looked stunned. Neil's face got strange then, as it will at such moments: it thickens. As if he has spirited himself away from the room at that moment, and left his empty face as a stand-in.

<hr>

HE SITS motionless beside me now, dreaming through the windshield. Daylight almost gone. Emptied out, both of us. Exhausted by words; sodden words shredded into fibrous strands, like wet tissue. The car is packed with silence, a sealed pod except when the seat creaks as I move my ass a notch to angle myself toward him. I can smell his deodorant, fake-pine, fake-ocean pong, and beneath that his own reassuring musk—sweetly oniony after a day's work, not at all unpleasant, in fact the opposite, in bed beneath him exciting, soothing—though we haven't had bed so often lately—his smooth skin, nubbly hair, his beating heart, the warmth under his wool shirt. Tonight he seems diminished, as he gazes off. I don't ask what he's thinking, as I long to, because the answer will be *Nothing*, and when he says the word he will mean it—baffled in fact, as though he'd ransacked his own skull that instant for any stray lint of thought, edged his fingertips across internal walls of seamless, shining bone. When I ask him how he thinks we're doing, he shrugs. If we seem to be having a good time, I point it out: *We seem to be having a good time.* His smile is vague; the implication, *nice try.*

It's as if I am trying to locate a certain key on an instrument, but the familiar button for it has vanished.

Him, no other. Hold on.

Others are going down around us, birds shot from the sky. People we know from around town, seemingly forever. Beautiful dark-haired Victoria Steele last year, early forties, mother of two, leukemia. Eleanor Willsworth, maybe thirty, vegan athlete and yoga queen, slender and quick, never smoked, lung cancer. Dave Walton, one of the attorneys I transcribe for, surfer and racquet-baller, dropped dead two Sundays ago while he was folding laundry and watching a football game, massive heart attack. Tom Bradley, a colleague of Neil's, finally got round to seeing a doc about some nuisance pain in his gut—stage three, it turns out. At such intervals a great stillness overtakes us. Neil's eyes go far away, and as I say, his long body seems to withdraw into itself.

My own eyes trace the outline of his cheek, his nose squared off at the tip, the caramel frizz, silvering all over, that he keeps cut so short now you can see his scalp through it. Imbedded, these details. I dream them. Sometimes in the dreams he romances another. In one, a strange woman lies full length on top of him at a party, belly to belly; he, supine, focuses a camera right at her face, inches away—all of it hotly erotic, vibrating, and I struggle to move through that heat to reach him, claim him—*you can stop that now, he is married to me*—but my limbs drag helplessly; my voice comes out scratchy, muffled. I wake panting.

Some moments I hate his spectacled face more than anything I can name, a murderous, consuming, dangerous hatred. It roars in my ears, soaks my vision, rockets down through the earth from my heart, legs, feet. The comprehension at such times, breathless with horror—*wasted, irretrievable, an entire life squandered*—unspoken, lest the ground open and gulp us like a bog hole—*you are the last person on earth I wish to be near at this moment; I wish you were on the other side of the world, I wish I'd never heard of you.* These moments are few but when upon us, strangle memory. Surely he's known them. Why are they so wild with rage? What do they portend?

Just now, though, it's the other way round. Long tall Neil feels foreshortened. The verities have reduced him. This is what happens when nature cuts men down. All their expensive science, their brisk good sense, no use. He looks into the distance as if he's just lost at a game he'd always, always won. The roulette of it teases both of us, ghoulishly, though no words pass between us: How long will the fates let him walk around whole, humming, rattling his grocery bags, calling out *Hi-ho* when he opens the front door? Anytime, anytime you named nowadays, I would gladly unzip his skin and climb inside and start sweeping and washing and dusting if it would plump him up again. Give us back our unthinking ease. Restore that thing we've so long been, part him, part me.

I can be pleased for this: there's no woman.

Instead, he says when Artie questions him, that I am not present enough. Not truly with him. That even when I am physically near I am somewhere else in my head, that he senses what I most want is to stay apart, be left alone with my books and papers. *You don't notice anything; you don't care, you don't listen,* he says. Instead, when I seem to be noticing or listening my eyes are coated with an opaque light, he says, as if I were also simultaneously listening to a secret radio station in my head. I don't care what I eat, he reminds Artie and me darkly. I don't take pains with food. I don't dry salad properly, I use too much dressing, I shake hot sauce and garlic salt on everything. I have *no awareness of the plate.*

Artie squints at him.

Neil goes on. I don't like his friends—I make this obvious, he says. He feels contaminated by it; he's begun to view them differently too, and it's my fault, my doing.

(I don't *dislike* them. They're kind people. I'd just—rather—use the time in other ways.)

It feels, he concludes, as if I am renting a room in his life.

Yes, I answer, my heart banging. But he is the one who owns the house.

Not the *house*, he fumes, darkening. The *life.*

There is plenty of truth in his accusations, and I can't pretend it does not shame me. He could make a spectacular courtroom show of it if he wanted, a tour de force. (Did you or did you not, on the night in question, shake hot sauce on my wild rice and blue cheese soufflé? Did you or did you not, in the conversation of a particular evening last week, call this or that acquaintance an idiot?) His friends, his food, his comings and goings—yes, yes— scaffolding I crouch behind, like something feral. But I never represented myself to him differently. And even if I'd meant to, how can I explain that there was never a good time for it? When exactly *is* a good time to say, *oh by the way, I hate cooking and most forms of social life?*

But my God (I plead with him) I'm aware of these things. Trying to be better. (Am I? In spirit, certainly.) And always thankful for him, ten thousand ways. This is true, and I tell him and tell him. Apparently, not enough. Or not the right way. Or rather, he says now, I've got to *show instead of tell*, the famous writers' axiom boomeranging back to thwack me in the neck.

He wants me to surprise him. Scout ahead. Bring back treasures. Arrange things.

Saran-wrapped at the front door? Oh, Christ.

No, he says, weary now. *Generate* something. Besides books.

Artie is squinting at Neil as if mulling one of those grade school math teasers. *If five people have one boat that only fits two, and can only cross the river twice—*

Part of me admires Neil's honesty. It can't be easy married to someone who'd rather live in pajamas, eat raisin bran—milk optional—who worries thieves might break into the car and steal her used copy of Mary Gordon. But meantime something's shifted, some pituitary awareness. I understand I can never quite trust him again in the old way, the way that felt so solid, so known. Steady as air, earth. Obviously I knew no such thing. I had persuaded myself; affixed the idea over comfortable years, like a smiley-face sticker. He has my attention now. It feels the way an actor's face looks when someone quickly runs a sword through him. *Malaise invaded; malaise can return.*

But what makes that such a big fat deal? I argue with myself. Never mind who'd care: what makes it different from the grand scheme? Crazy shit—and I don't mean pissy little Jamesian drawing-room slights, but atrocity—bombards folks with no warning every day; decent, forthright, shoelace-tying folks. If they *have* shoes. Look at Neil's clients; look at the news. Anything that's functioned, that's actually been good for us? Passable health, freedom from pain? Something to eat, clean water? Nobody pull a weapon today?

Frosting.

Rarely, I dream of living alone again. Single room, bed, desk, chair. One of those little box-sized refrigerators. Bare surfaces, calm light. A room painted white. Single daisy, maybe, in a bud vase. Rarely, I say, because in the next breath I know I'd freeze to death in that room, in two minutes. Curl up and mummify.

I put a hand on Neil's warm thigh. He pats it absently.

What I can't make him see, what I can't make him believe, is that if he is away for an evening—an evening!—I miss him with a sharpness that, again and again, knocks the wind from me. The house feels like a morgue. I marvel at my own barrenness, my zero-sum soul capital. It would never, ever occur to me to bake cookies, make soup, plant flowers, whap down the cobwebs with a flicked towel, call somebody on the phone. Shop, cook, shake-rattle-roll. Neil was born to draw people together. He loves nurseries, hardware stores. Buys paint and floor mats and ravioli-cutters. Plants impatiens and geraniums, rhododendrons, anything on sale. Brews his own limoncello (and it tastes better than store-bought). Invites folks round for no reason. *Bon vivant*-ism is a currency, a mandate, a motif—one of the million reasons he and Mike adored each other. Whereas I obey some equally ancient but opposing imprint, huddled in a ditch somewhere, shivering. I'd be stoned to death in another era, I'm completely aware of that, though it's not something I tend to bring up as table talk. My way recoils. His way steps forward with an extended hand, likely a glass of something delectable in it. Which do we seize on, when the airplane encounters the worst turbulence? What painting or poem places a loving hand on a terrified thigh?

I warm myself at the fire of my husband. A human hearth, Neil. If he's late from work or an errand I start to prowl the front window, and the first sight of his familiar outline through the glass flushes me with such relief I feel lightheaded. When I run into him by chance—it happened at the flu vaccine clinic last year—or see him laughing, his face accordioned, cheeks and nose reddening, brows sloped up in delicious helplessness; when he stares into the freezer, muttering; waters the plants with a drinking glass; when he reads, his specs throwing light so they look fogged, an index finger resting across an upper lip as if the finger were a routing device for the deepest currents of information; when he scampers through the house whooping, holding in both hands like a torch the *New Yorker* he knows I want—

When he fills the kitchen with greasy bowls and ziplock bags, making gallons of turkey stock—

At those times, I can't be married *enough* to him.

Now I feel him gliding slowly off, as if on an ice floe.

Please, Neilly. Please don't take yourself away.

At last he stirs. He looks tired.

"Shall we?"

*W*ith little grunts we unfold from the car, take steps across the gravel-salted asphalt. It's *l'heure bleu*. Sky inking, air ribboned with the hills' moist sweetness, a faint scent of turned earth entwined with car exhaust. As we near, I hear adult voices, laughter, clinking glasses. Beneath that, guitar, Brazilian, so gentle it makes my eyes smart.

We spot Addie at the opposite end of the room in a snug navy suit, matching pumps, and a single strand of seed pearls against her flawless throat, so simple and elegant that she could have been born wearing them. She looks like an international airline hostess, startling amidst the unbathed aging hippies and bikers in their down vests and plaid flannel and leather chaps. What's striking this time is the careful conventionality of her beauty, the kind of thirtyish woman earning second looks in airports and financial districts, the whole out-of-reach magazine-model force field. She is talking with admirers. Tilda flanks her daughter like some florid bisexual valet, wearing a maroon pants-and-shirt getup resembling medical scrubs. Behind the two of them an archway opens to the topaz of the hotel pool, lit from beneath by the golden eyes of underwater sconces. Steam spirals from the water's surface in the chill. And look: there is little Harry, circling Addie like a hyped-up moon—Chet's brown hair, Addie's brown eyes changed from their smoke-blue birth color. He tugs at his mother, fruitlessly, then darts suddenly straight for us, whooshing between Neil and me with millimeters to spare, as if by sonar. He wears red lederhosen, embroidered on the chest with what appears to be a scuttling goose; hard to be sure—the boy's shot past that fast.

Neil heads at once for Addie and Tilda. Since I am linked to him at the upper arm, I travel along like a sidecar. He veers toward Tilda's arms; I un-link. They embrace without a word. Tilda's eyes close. Addie and I observe them a moment; then I turn to her.

"Addie."

I must stand on tiptoe—I'd forgotten how tall she is, and what a slender waist!—to kiss her cheek. Her delicate scent engulfs me, subtle as orchid.

"Addie, you smell so lovely. I remember this scent from the night you visited. Will you tell me what it is, so I can try to find it?"

She is pleased. "Vera Wang," she says firmly. A woman in her position will own a library of scents; be able, with no preliminaries, to cite each and discuss their merits like a scholar.

I nod, making a show of it. "It's wonderful. I'll look for it. In any good department store? Thank you." (And I will undertake a special trip to Macy's to try it, assisted by sheet-white young girls with black lips, and on my wrist it will smell like funeral carnations.)

Addie smiles, chatting calmly. I see no evidence on her enchanting face of recent tears, or lost sleep, lost anything. But that is not fair, because she has had many weeks, before this, to do whatever it is Addie does with her feelings. After I have asked after Chet and the business and New Mexico life (fine, happy, doing well), I don't know what else to say. We have no common life except for Mike, and for some reason, despite the occasion, saying predictable things to her about her deceased father feels intrusive, and clumsy, and late. But I am spared because Neil has turned to Addie. Her eyes brighten and she opens her arms. He's one of the few people taller than her in this room.

"Uncle Neil!" She sighs with unconcealed gladness as they hug, and I am forced to confront Tilda.

"Tilda, how are you?"

I take her shoulders: flesh that gives, like pudding. I press my cheek to hers. As usual it is damp, her breath yeasty. Would it be meds or booze or both, that make her sweat so?

I step back, look at her. Her face noncommittal. She could be waiting for a bus.

"Tilda, are you okay? How is it going?"

"Peachy," she says, eyeing the room. "This music sucks, don't you think?"

The sound system has switched, preposterously, to the theme song from *American Bandstand*. But people don't seem to mind: they shout and laugh; alcohol doing its reliable work. Harry careens around and between the adults, making *vroom-vroom* sounds. On its surface the gathering has mustered a scratchy cheer, like fizz on ginger ale.

⸎

THE GROUP around the silver tub of iced beers (many tubs placed throughout the room, alongside chafing dishes of charbroiled Polish sausages and sourdough buns, Mike's favorites)—in a glance I know them: Neil's dinner crew from the old days, the lawyers, the actors, the mechanics, the teachers. Janna, the self-ordained minister, wears a red and black serape; she's just got back from a silence retreat at a hot springs, her narrow face goofy with knowingness; Ted, the much-divorced contractor, wears his canary-swallowing leer. I learned long ago he had nothing in particular to leer about; it's just the default expression he wears. And Dustin, the mime who eats millet seed: I can glimpse his shaved head floating behind the gang as usual, smiling, solicitous as a butler. Dustin teaches stilt-walking and juggling; he lives on a pallet in someone's garage. For years I assumed him a savant, like Prince Myshkin. He seemed to ask nothing for himself; you wanted to heat him up some soup. But I changed my thinking one day when I saw him make his way through a crowd and he didn't know I was watching. His face seemed fixed on an urgent errand beyond the setting; I watched him cleave through people

- 129 -

as if pushing rats off a life raft. It was ambition I was seeing: raw, exposed, cold as steel. Ambition for what, who can say. Money? A woman? Better quality millet? True, one sees it everywhere: bald striving, inside hierarchies that denounce striving. Power struggles at the Zen Center. But I remember wondering: How much else have I misread in perfect, serene confidence—for how long, and how badly?

Mike's skuzzbag biker pals stand around, bellies shelfing out like sandwich meat between leather vests and stud-belted jeans. An old biker seems a visual non sequitur; the image so childishly stubborn you want to laugh. Discounting Addie and Harry, hair on the heads in this room adds up to far more salt than pepper; skin is mottled, saggy and lined. The old dinner crew roars a greeting as Neil approaches—relieved for fortification they can recognize, a fellow parachutist. He grins, nods as he ambles toward them. Some hard inner piece of me softens to see his pleasure. I drift away.

This Hilton understands nothing, certainly, about lighting. White brick walls, white fluorescent tubes overhead, effect of a prison hospital. I pluck a beer from the nearest tub of snow and wander to a long table near the entrance. It is covered with pressed white linen; memorabilia have been placed the length of it, evenly spaced, like exhibits at a fair. Photographs, articles. Mike in his Navy uniform and cap, stiff, attentive, his naked-chinned face moistly young. Mike beside his Black Beast, outfitted in black leather. Framed certificates: the Association of Zoos and Aquariums, *Michael Field Spender*. (These had been nowhere evident in the Albuquerque apartment.) Here at last are the photo albums, bulky and stiff, capillaries of dark green mold blooming under their cellophane. Baby shots of Mike, baby shots of Addie, Addie's wedding, newborn Harry, toddler Harry—a ringer, I'm reminded, for toddler Mike. Lifetimes skimmed in seconds. Drive-by lives. No photos of the young Tilda—except the one in which she sits with Mike at someone's desk, glaring back at the photographer.

I pick up a small photo, creased black and white with scalloped edges: a twenty-year-old Mike wearing only a straw hat and trunks, grinning, stick-lean, barefoot, posed on a fishing skiff in the sun. Palm trees in the background. Sea surface glittering. Skinny but muscled—you can count his ribs.

A very strange enchanted boy.

A man in a suit hovers next to me, flipping through album pages. Pawing at tokens, as I am. The way you'd flip through old record covers, poster prints. A flea market, an estate sale. Something pornographic about it. I don't feel well. Dreading the man beside me—he could turn at any moment to speak to me. I edge away from the table. There can only be one opening line at a gathering like this, and I cannot bear it. I've run out of good will, run out of certainty or even the will to fake certainty; can no longer let my face lapse into that rictus of goodgirlness so automatic I sometimes feel my face still frozen into it at night before sleep: mouth pinched up, eyes crinkling as they would at strangers in supermarket aisles, at walkers crossing streets. It's a thing women do, that inane fusion of apology with twit-headed cheer. Women apologize, with a stricken smile, if you purposefully step on their feet. We're sorry all the time, sorry for time itself, for ourselves, for you, for the pains of existence, for unaccountable evil. We're sorry and we want to make it better, for everyone. That's what the sick smile means, a first law of femaleness. Children wonder at this falsity. As do women themselves. It confuses us and breaks our hearts because we're only trying to be good, damn it to fucking hell. Be good, do good, but if we thought about it a half-minute we'd have to concede it never does any good. At night I work to make this face let go. When I do, it feels like an empty bag.

⁂

IT IS an odd noise which tweaks me from my brooding (*Ms. Miseryguts*, Neil used to call it). Behind the music's inanity—a muzak version of "Hello, Dolly"—comes a white noise I can't identify at first, followed by a woman's scream. Not a scream like in the movies; more a gasp, a surprised, sucking-in sound. Almost an inhaled question. *Haaaghh?* The crowd repeats the sound. There is more confused sound and then a general movement toward it; before I've registered these elements the herd is funneling itself across the room murmuring in alarm, toward the archway at the other end. I crane my neck, cursing my height, trying to see around bodies and heads. Addie and Tilda have disappeared, and so has Neil.

I hear two more quick explosions of the mysterious noise, and now I recognize the sound. Water splashes, cannonball-sized.

Without knowing why, I know Neil's in the water. I push toward the pool through pressing bodies, not bothering to excuse myself. Torsos seem to fatten and interlock around me; I shove hard against the spongy middles, reeking aftershave and cologne and body odors, the rough of wool, the muddy give of leather.

Neil never learned to swim.

"Let me through! Let me through! My husband's out there. My husband!" Panic squeezes my lungs; my shoves grow violent. I hold one arm straight out like a ship's prow and use the other like a rudder, elbowing.

"Whoa, little missy," someone grunts, his breath wafting beer fumes.

I emerge at the curved lip of the pool, past the crowd's mutterings, in time to find Neil standing in the shallow end to his waist; in time to see his long paws handing up to Addie the dripping but unharmed (and plainly delighted) little Harry, red suspenders now looping from his soaked outfit: the whole ballet underlit by sconce lights from beneath the water, the boy's eyelashes stuck together in black starry points all round his wide brown eyes. Addie gathers the child to her, peeved but not at all unhinged; she's been taking Harry to toddler swim lessons, it turns out, since he could walk. Beside Neil in the water stands Tilda, who must have dived instead of jumped, as he did. Her hair is pasted to her skull; her medical scrubs cling to her blocky form, her breasts seem pancaked, bandaged flat. Two hotel flunkies rush toward Addie and Harry with armfuls of towels and expressions of anguish. In a beat the three adults have bundled the child in a towel and are shepherding him off to Addie's room. Harry's little legs hustle double-time beside the grownup legs, steam curling from his shining head as he chatters in a high clear voice: "I didn't mean to, Mama, but it was fun! Did you see me, Mama? Did you?"

I have not stated, before this, that I love to swim. Not a pro, but devoted. All year, days or evenings, rain or fair. From since I was a kid, when I spent entire summers at the municipal pool, the phony turquoise of pool water beckons to me; the scent of chlorine stirs and soothes. I have a secret idea that water rearranges you inside, if only temporarily. Wakes you from duller states, shunts you all at once into a different dream, like a trap door opening and suddenly you weigh very little and the medium is viscous, clear, and warm, and you can fly along with no effort on your belly or your back. I'm tempted to jump in now just to keep Neil company, but something warns me to hold still.

Neil and Tilda stand side by side, looking blankly at the retreating Harry, then at each other, their shadows wibble-wobbling sideways across the pool floor. Neil's still wearing his wool jacket: its bottom edges float out from him like petals. Nets of droplets twinkle over his jacket sleeves, his hair. Steam drifts from Tilda. In the blue-gold underwater light their lower bodies are stubby blurs, as if only the top halves of them remain.

It's bright as day what they're thinking.

Would Mike love this.

In unison they burst out laughing. They double over, Neil's hands on his underwater knees for support, and the relieved crowd assembled at poolside also begins to laugh, uncertain. Then after an invisible moment, like the last scarlet wink of sun folding into green ocean, Tilda's laughter turns to tears. It's like watching the comedy mask melt into the tragedy mask, her face wadding, a twisted-up rag. Neil takes her in his arms and stands with her in the blue-gold water while she sobs.

$\mathscr{M}$artinis are gasoline, after all.

No matter the fancy olives. No matter the fragile cranberry or apricot or green-apple color, not even, this time, the tiny, carved, raw ginger goldfish. No matter what you toss in there. I left that drink behind in my thirties—days of revving in place, handsome and strong and hopeful and completely ignored, eating pizza and drinking martinis in North Beach bars. (Except once, an older man walked up and said, *You look like a Porsche on a dirt road*.) How I got home safely after those stubborn experiments still fills me with wonder. Some roaming Grace swooped a wing over me. When you think of all the lives sucked down that rabbit hole—oh, how lucky I was.

So I volunteered to drive us all home that spring night in Albuquerque: our last night with the Spenders as it would turn out; our last night with Mike in his life. The night of the oyster bar.

Resolved, remember, to make myself beloved. I can drive anything, so the different car didn't worry me. It seemed the other three had expected my offer, even hinted at it—the intent way they looked at me when the waiter asked for my order, since they know me to be the lightweight among drinking friends. Cajun fiddles sizzling up the place made a body reckless; air of a fog-bound seacoast bar, briny with woe—good trick for a shanty in the high desert, outskirts of a university campus. I asked for a beer and glass of water. We sat around a wooden cable spool: Mike, Tilda, Neil and me, surrounded by dirt-creased vagrants and pierced, tattooed students at other spool tables.

Once I'd offered, the other three smiled and got busy. The first tray appeared. Small goldfish floated in their glass pedestals, flesh-pink carvings—ingenious, really—preserved in clear lighter fluid. Neil gave me his to eat. The aftertaste made my eyes water.

Middle of the afternoon. Coolish and cloudy outside, dark and steamy with idle breath inside. Zydeco fiddle and accordian had taken over thought waves, a waltz on the speaker system. I tasted my beer. Cajun music really does sound like sawing. But it seeps into you, stately, sad, stinging your eyes like barbecue smoke. *One* two three, *one* two three. *Oh* (two, three) *Pop* (two three), *tu me parle toujours; tu me parle dans tes chansons.*

My three grew boisterous, shouted and laughed; Mike's booming HA! made a bass percussion against the fiddles and accordions. Two dozen raw oysters arrived, with little dishes of tabasco, sweet vinegar, horseradish.

Neil stood up, a dripping shell in his hand. He waited till our eyes settled on him, lifted it.

"My good friends—my good wife," he added, smiling at me.

It's a complicated smile: *Don't fuck this up.*

"To good life," he added. He gazed at his friends.

Tilda raised a brimming shell, pleased. Mike's eyes glittered.

I lifted my own shell, its slimy cargo dosed with tabasco.

After a beat or two, Mike was able to let loose a yell. "HA!"

We tilted and slurped. *Ooooh yeah*, sang the zydeco band. Tilda slipped an oyster down Mike's gullet. Then another, and another. For a moment he shape-shifted before my eyes, into a sea lion bull. Then Mike's eyes welled up.

Oh, Jesus. Here we go.

Tilda, as usual, didn't act the least bothered, slurping up the silver-edged lumps, incising with her teeth the delicate ligaments that tethered them to their shells.

I couldn't ignore Mike's tears.

"Mikey? What is it, Mikey? You okay? Everything okay?"

Water zigzagged along his face's creases as he labored to form the words.

"Only—how to—make it . . . *stay*."

It took him what felt like years to get that last word out.

He meant us. We were here because he had asked Tilda for us. Mike believed in us, I saw then—saw it, somehow, for the first time. His great pools of eyes weren't only upon me in sexual reflex. I don't know why it had taken me so long to comprehend that, and it still makes me unhappy to think about. Believed and loved without complexity or qualification, and this quality must have been true of him all their lives together, Neil's and Tilda's with him, long before the stroke. He took no part in Tilda's casual, corrosive irony. He had nothing like that in him.

"That's cool, Mike," I said. "That's a nice way to say it."

I reached for his good hand, dark pink and warm, and held it between both of mine, patting it. I glanced at the others. Tilda wore her vacant, so-what face, scanning the room as if massively bored. Her one-purpose-fits-all expression, popped open like an umbrella.

Neil's face had quieted.

Yeeee-hah wailed the zydeco singers; fiddle sliding away, dutiful, pliant. Smells of fried meat, sticky alcohol.

I released Mike's hand and, in a sudden inspiration, leaned toward Tilda.

"Tilda, how did you grow up?"

I felt Neil's glance, but would not look at him. Heaven knows I've glued my pleading silent eyeballs on him often enough, praying he might get the message and slow his eating, or that my kick to his shin would clamp off whatever ill-timed words were that moment prancing out of his mouth. Besides: *reversing the energy* was my game. Shouldn't it be obvious? Getting onto her side. Being pro-active, for fuck's sake.

Also, she was drinking truth serum.

She stopped laughing and stared at me, eyes still wet from laughing. I watched her face muscles slowly fall, like my question was a pile of unpaid bills she'd just uncovered. She took a swallow from her glass—a little ginger fish bobbed to its edge to kiss her. She picked it out and tossed it, licked her fingers.

"Who wants to know?"

I noticed for the first time that her nose seemed to have been shoved back into her face. Maybe someone decked her once. Hardly a stretch to imagine.

"Me." I pumped a lilt into my voice, my brows. "No hidden cameras, no microphones." Hands aloft.

The music had picked up, a lazy two-step, rhythm of kicking rocks while you walked. One two, kick. If I listened I could make out the slangy French. The singer's car has broken down on the way to her wedding. *Si j'arrange pas ce sacré char, je vais être tard pour mon enterrement.* If I don't get this damned car fixed, I'll be late for my own funeral.

Three fresh martinis appeared, the emptied glasses stacked noisily on a tray and carted off. I was thinking how Tilda would feel tomorrow—the awful pressure in the brain, the hatpin piercing of the temples, the blurred thought, aching eyeballs, taste like shit in the mouth. Then it occurred to me she probably woke up feeling that way most days for many years now. Tilda belonged to a league I couldn't really know except by joke and hearsay, to whom the word *breakfast* holds automatic equivalency with *hair of the dog*.

"Not what you'd suppose," she said, startling me. I'd not expected any reply. I don't really know what I expected. Her smile was twisted, and something about its crookedness threw a light, like a trick door cracking open, a door you hadn't known existed. For a moment I regretted my bravado, and was afraid.

"Not what anyone supposes," she said, studying her plate of empty wet shells.

The Kralls first owned one of those ritzy showcase homes in the Oakland hills. Montclair: Not many knew about the area then, and those who did kept it quiet; in those days so woodsy and lush most of the homes were almost completely hidden from a visitor's eyes, roads more like paths, full of tortured turns. Only the random mailbox sticking out from the lush conifers and boxwood gave any clue that people lived somewhere back there. Now and again you'd come upon a fancy car parked half off the rutted way, say a cream-colored roll-top Cadillac convertible, gleaming—so absurd against that setting it seemed a mirage, or somehow airlifted to the spot. But once you arrived at the Kralls' place (by a more overgrown drive), the house opened out before you. A long, horseshoe-shaped, ranch-style affair—style of the times. Three-car garage. Many bedrooms, sunken fireplace, maid, cook, gardener.

"The place was probably a prison to my mother," Tilda said. "She rattled around in it. Even though we were little we could tell she was miserable. It seemed like she never ate. She was always looking for two things, I remember: her cigarettes and her tranquilizers."

Tilda remembered a set of large Japanese dolls in individual glass cases, lined up along the fireplace mantle. These weren't babies or toddler dolls but mature women in elaborate kimonos and sashes: gleaming black hair in balloonish arrangements framing white faces. Smiles imperceptible. Slits for eyes. Tiny rectangle mirrors dangled from pins in their hair, each in a different costume in her oblong glass booth. Their gazes were self-erasing, despite all the costumery. Relics of Mr. Krall's war years. The dolls were never to be touched.

"I wanted those dolls," Tilda said. "Oh man, did I want 'em." She shook her head, turning her glass by its stem. "What good was a doll you couldn't play with?"

The tiny mirrors shivered, glittering, she remembered, if you touched the dolls' cases. "I used to drag one of the heavy wooden dining chairs over and stand on it for a closer look, when nobody was around."

Mr. Krall—a man whose stomach preceded him into a room—ran the East Bay headquarters of a company that made cardboard boxes. When you got in on certain things on the ground floor, the rest became gravy, as he liked to remind his family (leaning back after a heavy meal, when Tilda would notice the wet oblongs in the armpits of his shirt). After a certain point he hadn't much real work to do, because his company had been purchased by a larger one, and that in turn by a larger one, and nobody had yet been fired—an era before downsizing. So Chester Krall often punched in, left the building and drove down to the city to join a bunch of regulars for many hours at certain bars along the Embarcadero—reporters, teamsters, other displaced members of middle management. He'd return to his office in the late afternoon, punch out, make a few more stops and arrive home long past dinner, usually after everyone else was in bed. He would have a drink, eat the foil-wrapped meal the cook had left out for him, look at the mail, watch a bit of TV before turning in, though most often he passed out fully dressed on the couch. These habits caused Lucille Krall, a bony neurasthenic woman who made them all go to church Sundays and made the little girls wear white gloves each time, to grow quieter as the maid served her and the girls their late afternoon tomato bisque and filet of sole. The silence of those early dinners, with only the occasional clink of fork against plate, was excruciating for Tilda—"like no air," she murmured. Afterward Mrs. Krall would retire to her bedroom "to rest" and close the door; the girls could hear her slamming drawers at her vanity table. Matilda and her older sister Elise were not allowed to ask about their father's activities.

Tilda had a sister?

"Oh yeah," she grunted. "Leesie. We don't speak anymore."

The zydeco soundtrack had at last subsided, and no one bothered to replace it. Another tray of martinis appeared, their predecessors cleared but the sticky table unwiped. Neil had begun to look pale and glassy; at length he rose, bumping his chair a good distance; it shrieked as it scraped the cement floor. He pulled one of the Cuban stogies from his shirt pocket, examined it, glanced longingly at Mike. But Mike had gone to sleep, head crooked sideways onto shoulder, lips wet with spittle, exactly like an exhausted child in a high chair. A snore soughed from his mouth and nose; his lips *pupp-pupp-pupping* softly from their wet center as the air escaped them. Neil mumbled about finding the loo before having his smoke outside, and set off.

So where did Elise live?

"Still camps in my mother's apartment. Works for the City of Oakland, one of those lifer secretaries. Chain smokes. Peculiar bitch. Spends more time with her parakeets than with people. Mario and Lily. She may as well have given birth to them. Played this tape for them again and again, trying to teach 'em to talk. Drive you plumb-ass nuts."

Tilda mimicked the tape, its exaggerated elocution.

"*Hel-lo, bay-beee, want a kiss?* Over and over. Those dumb birds only cheeped and chittered. Leesie never could stay hooked up with anybody, big surprise. Way outclassed my mother in the peculiarity department."

Tilda spoke without affect. Though she answered questions as I put them to her she seemed to be talking to herself, never actually looking at me but keeping her eyes closed as she spoke; when she did open them she seemed to fix them on an invisible zone just behind the plates and glasses—there's no other way to describe it—where a crystal ball might have sat, as if she were narrating a series of miniature enactments she watched unfurl there. You could argue it was only the gin, but I had the eeriest sense she had lowered herself into a sort of trance, and was responding to my prompts from some deep, buffered dream state. She kept turning her martini glass by its stem, round and round.

Chester Krall apparently died suddenly, in 1967, and it took the two girls several years to find out he had died in the arms of one of his mistresses. An aneurysm. It was Elise who'd finally prised the facts from their increasingly prescription-doped mother. "Just like some trashy headline," Tilda said with a short, hard laugh. Krall had apparently owed a lot of money, left their finances in bad shape—"for a festive little door prize," Tilda said. At first Lucille couldn't believe their money situation because they'd always lived so well; she was eventually persuaded by the attorney Krall's company sent over (by way of an official gesture of sympathy that would also ease the firm out from future liability). With the attorney's help she sold the Montclair house; with what slender profit remained she paid most of Krall's debts and bought a three-room Oakland apartment. There the two girls and their mother lived on a miniscule pension until Lucille's death eight years later—but according to Tilda, "it was no kind of life." She fled when Lucille died, in 1977. Tilda was seventeen.

Tilda scratched her ear, resumed turning the glass stem. "I never found out what happened to those fucking dolls," she said to it, amused.

Apparently Lucille adored firstborn Elise, whose manners and nature, according to Tilda, were "ultra-fem." Leesie knew how to enhance her mother's devotion. She wore frilly outfits, cultivated long blonde curls. Lucille spent hours combing and setting the girl's hair; Tilda remembers baskets of rollers, papers, clips, and mega-sized jars of setting gel, clear baby-pink and baby-blue goo like jello, or clear icing. (Tilda tasted the gels once, lifting the jars from the bathroom cupboard, touching a fingertip to each color and to her tongue—a taste, she said, like soapy pennies.) Elise would sit at her mother's vanity table, brought with them from the Montclair house. It had a ruffle of blue-green plaid tacked around its edges that fell to the floor. "I still remember the tacks that held that ruffle in place," Tilda said. "They were faceted, as if little thumbs had made prints in each facet, dark metal like distressed brass work. I spent a lot of time staring at them." She liked hiding inside the ruffle and butting Leesie's legs with her head, meowing, infuriating her sister. Mother and eldest daughter sipped lemonade or hot cocoa while Lucille combed and pinned, chatting; Leesie would bow her head slightly in a stiff way, eyes on herself in the mirror. Whereas Tilda could not bear holding still, yelled and twisted whenever Lucille tried to brush her hair, until Lucille threatened to "bop" her on the skull with the tortoiseshell back of the hairbrush, her voice a shrill rasp. *I'm gonna bop you.* And sometimes she would do it; she'd crack Tilda on the head. Tilda would tear out the door in her dirty jeans, holing up in secret places. Her favorite was a space in an alleyway between two buildings; a large heating and ventilation unit created a small protected area, and a couple of stripling trees broke through the asphalt to form a sort of curtain. There she'd once traded vagina-for-penis viewings with a neighbor boy (she was unimpressed, reminded of the cocktail sausages her parents had served at the Montclair parties). But she'd also hidden treasure there—a cigar box winnowed from someone's trash, stashed under a nest of extruding pipes. In the box she collected many lengths of telephone cable wires; each wire sheathed in malleable plastic of a different rainbow color. She'd find the wire clippings in mounded deposits, like exotic scat, at certain construction sites. You could bend the wires into shapes of animals and stars, braid them, make rings or a crown. As long as the weather held, she spent many soothing hours with her bendable wires, adorning herself, creating wire families. When the child returned home and demanded some of the lemonade or cocoa on view, Lucille would tell her those were "only for well-behaved little girls."

Tilda remembered, after one such refusal, marching to her mother's bedroom; she dropped her jeans and defecated on her mother's handmade Turkish throw carpet.

She glanced at me—her glance during this recitation never actually met my eyes; and when I tried to glimpse her own eyes they seemed to be covered with silver, or so I fancied, though anyone could of course insist it was the alcohol; but all of it only reinforced my sense of her trancelike state—and she laughed, a mirthless bark. "I can't remember how she punished me that time. I must've blocked it out."

One day, Lucille told the girls they were going for a special treat to Schrafft's, then a favorite ice cream parlor in San Francisco.

They had to dress up, was the catch. Scratchy tulle. Black patent pumps.

"Leesie was tormenting me while we got ready. About wearing the right stuff, the way I looked, fuck knows what. She called me a toad, called me Quasimodo."

Tilda gave a twisted grin. "We'd seen that movie on TV on Saturday afternoon, kiddie-scary movie hour. *Shock Theater*, it was called. Anyway, I slugged her," she said.

She'd punched her big sister in the face, and after much howling and rushing about by Lucille and applications of cold water and ice, a satisfying purple-blue ring manifested around one of Leesie's pretty green eyes.

Lucille—by then in heaven knew what kind of psychic or physical shape—locked her youngest daughter in the girls' bedroom closet. It was a small closet, not much larger than a phone booth, with a single upper shelf and dirty clothes on the floor, utterly black with the door sealed. All that could be seen from inside were two pinpoints of light where the screws held the doorknob in place, and the thread of daylight where the door met the concrete floor. The closet required a key to lock, which Lucille, with frenzied determination, had located in her own room and then, having wrestled the screaming child into the space and slammed the door, inserted and turned. Tilda yelled and cried and begged to be let out; she pulled and pummeled the doorknob until her hands were bruised. The clothes and laundry and shoes above and around and beneath her seemed to muffle her cries, which poured back muted into her own ears together with the sound of her pounding heart, as if she were wearing padded earphones listening to a recording of herself.

Lucille took Elise and her purse, and left the apartment.

My own heart, I suddenly noticed, was also pounding; my stomach tight. I couldn't fathom Tilda's face, her eyes closed or staring, by turns, at the crystal-ball zone.

"Jesus Christ, Tilda," I said.

"I'll never know for sure how long they were gone. Couple hours maybe," she said. Sitting with her knees drawn up, the girl kept her eyes on the pinpoints of light where the doorknob screws pierced the wood, the thread line of light, bluish, at the door's bottom. Now and again she grabbed parts of herself to be sure she was still there in the dark; feet, knees, elbows—pressed her fingers to her cheeks, neck, scalp, eyelids. She experimented with curling up on her side embryo-style, then on her back with her knees up. It smelled like old shoe leather in there, dirty socks, attic dust. After awhile she decided it might be good to sing. She sang anything she could remember: Oh say can you see, Bloody Mary is the girl I love, There was a farmer had a dog and Bingo was his name. She sang television commercials, Munch, munch, munch a bunch of Fritos—corn chips. Over and over. And she thought about things.

"I thought about my favorite television shows, about who I liked and who I hated at school. Mostly I thought about running away," she said, turning her empty glass. She plotted her escape with all the details she could foresee or recall. She would slip some bills from her mother's wallet—easily accomplished; done it many times—to get a bus ride as far toward the ocean as it could take her. She would hitchhike the rest of the way, get herself to Bodega Bay—the family had visited once, a day trip when their father was alive. He'd taken them for clam chowder, with packets of little hexagonal oyster crackers. Once there, she would live in an abandoned shack. Or she would build one out of driftwood. She could get a job on a salmon trawler, eat fish they caught. Maybe she could wash dishes in the diner where they ate clam chowder that time.

"And?" I said at length, after she'd lapsed into silence.

A downstairs neighbor, an elderly woman, though accustomed to shouting matches from the mysterious upstairs widow and her daughters, had been alarmed by the sustained howls of the girl, followed by a silence that frightened her even more; and after an hour of indecision she summoned police, who broke into the apartment and closet, and freed Tilda—the girl astonished to be greeted by uniformed men wearing badges. ("That might have been the only time in my life I've been glad to see cops," she said.) They gave her a glass of Lucille's off-limits pineapple juice and asked her questions very gently, as if she were a newborn puppy, which fascinated her. They were still there talking with Tilda when Lucille, ashen, walked in the opened, splintered front door with Elise. The cops then had a conversation with Lucille, the gist of which, apparently, was a mild remonstration.

I held my hands to my cheeks.

"But—what about child protection? Social services?"

Tilda shook her head. In those days, she said, there was no child protection agency, and social services were only called in for the most extreme cases.

She shrugged. "Your kids were basically considered your property, short of something like murder."

It occurred to me then that I had reached a ceiling of incredulousness—my empathy, like a balloon, had begun to subtly deflate. I'd exhausted the kind of anxious attention one spends in listening with care, perhaps too long, to another's ordeal, with the sad inverse result that, as the ordeal takes on more appalling dimensions, the amount of care (visible on one's face, unless one is a very good actress) decreases instead of accelerating. A notion nagged at me that what I was hearing, under Tilda's gin-induced spell, amounted to another form of braggadocio, another see-you-one-and-raise-you-one, but this time in the misfortune category. This is not to say I did not believe what Tilda was telling me. I believed it all too well. I just felt weirdly, overwhelmingly tired.

"Anyway, after that we all kind of went dead on each other," she continued. When Lucille died, at fifty-two, of congestive heart failure, Tilda agreed that Leesie would stay on in their mother's apartment, and hopped onto the back of a high school pal's motorcycle to travel north. She headed straight for Bodega, as childhood fantasy had dictated, and tried to carve an existence there for a year or so. But after she'd wearied of washing dishes and cleaning houses (and learned she wasn't pretty enough to get hired to wait tables where the tip money mattered) and seeing that no other real work would be found there, wandered further up the old arterial highway (not a freeway yet) to the sleepy, rose-and-ocean-scented enclave called Mira Flores. She wanted to find the Porthole bar, a place her biker friends had talked so much about. But first she walked over to the Legal Aid office a few doors down, and asked for a job. She spoke some Spanish, she told the long-haired workers. She could type and file, answer phones, run errands.

Also, she told them, she had a certain ability to connect with the underdog.

It might, she said, come in handy.

- IV -

Two months after the memorial gathering, April, Saturday afternoon. Early spring, the light delicate as skim milk. I am reading; Neil's at the gym. The phone rings. I let the machine answer, and wait to hear who's phoning.

"Yo, sweeties! Tilda Spender here—"

I hasten to the machine, seize the receiver, stab my finger at the connecting button. Infuriating—it always takes a couple of stabs.

"Tilda! Tilda for God's sake, we've been trying forever to get hold of you."

Aware at once, abashed for it—my own casual, impossible wealth—the world-assuming, universe-assuming, both-alive-in-real-time *we*.

I perch at the edge of the bed. The precise spot Neil sat when he wept, months ago—a different planet ago; other people ago. Out the window the privet tree is alive with robins, orange-red breasts fat as human fists, flapping and flittering, falling off and re-alighting, making party music—high-pitched, staccato giggling. They eat the tree's purple-black berries, cascades of them—the birds dangling upside down to snatch at them, flapping crazily to keep their grip on the sagging branches. They get drunk, fly reckless, laughing and hollering, shitting explosive, purple-black arcs onto the back steps and house walls. The sky is filled, reeling with them.

"How have you been, Tilda? What're you doing? *Where* are you?"

"In my kitchen, sweeties! Crying, singing, having a fuck of a time. Got Mike's ashes here right in front of me. Scooping up spoonfuls. Putting a couple spoons into little ziplock bags. Thought I'd send bits of his ashes out to all his friends. Want some?"

My vision abandons the robin-fest. I can see her in the Albuquerque kitchen.

Standing at the counter. Pink gin fizz at her elbow, milky scum coating the empty part of the glass. Half-empties and empties (beer, champagne, tequila, Beefeater, Stoly, Yaeger, schnapps) lining the countertop like multicolored organ pipes. The radio's on. She is weeping, singing with and without the radio, spooning dark ash from the box or jar or whatever the crematorium has shipped them in—into ziplock sandwich bags fanned out along the tile counter. An assembly line. I can make out the music in the background: "Under the Boardwalk." She sings under her breath through the receiver while I'm speaking: "down by the seeeeeee, yeah yeah yeah." She is blitzed. I can guess she has not bathed or washed her hair for some time, there at her countertop, spooning her spoonfuls, greasy and rank with sweat and ash.

I slide from the bed to the floor holding the receiver, prop my forehead on an arm across my knees. The afternoon light pearling and still—except for the careening, fluffy bodies, the demented *tee-hee-hee-hee-hee-hee* rails outside as robins wheel and dive.

She's held onto those ashes a while. Maybe she couldn't face them before this.

But the idea of a baggie of Mike's ashes arriving in the mail makes me queasy. Would Neil really want them? What would we do with them? For some reason I envision them as dark gray, though it goes against sense. I saw a dog's ashes once: its owner kept them in a Tupperware container in his closet, a kind of homage. They were ivory-colored, smooth and dry, like different size pebbles. I have no idea whether Neil will care about getting some of Mike's ashes, but he's not home to ask.

I study my bare feet.

"Tilda, are you okay? What are you doing now?"

"Same, same. Doing the deli job, seeing my grandson. Pick him up from school every day. Yesterday we went to the Living Desert Museum—heard of it? We saw a two-headed thing: snake, scorpion, lizard, God knows. Harry's telling me all about the thing. Chapter and verse, man; yammering on like some high school biology teacher. Kid's awesome. No fear on earth in him."

I hope she doesn't drive the boy around with too much booze in her. But Addie would be keeping an eye on that.

Wouldn't she?

I flex my toes. Reasonable to assume Tilda would cork the bottles for the duration of babysitting, at least. That child is everything to her now.

But when has Tilda ever been reasonable?

"For a while he was scotch-taping signs to everything in the house. Table, Chair, Mirror. Then he started taping them to us."

I can hear her breath between spoken words, humming while breathing.

"Dad, Mom, and me—Gramma Tee—that's what he calls me, Gramma Tee. Very amusing, wearing our labels around. But now he's taken his little project outside, taping signs to rocks and trees and plants—but get this, with the *scientific names* for them. The *Latin*, would you believe."

She pauses, humming tunelessly through her nostrils. I wonder whether she's popped an upper to counteract the booze.

"Tilda, hey, that's great. Wow. You must be so proud. That's just—great."

Whose words are these? I sound like a kid selling cookies.

"You know we think about you a lot, Tilda. We really—we hope you're okay."

Weak, trite words. And *we, we, we*. But what others to summon?

The words are partly true. Everything is partly true. That's the confounding thing. But energies wane earlier now. So does the quality of belief we used to carry around like banners—a color-fast constant that held, wash after wash. You want to tell certain people, *Oh please, just be all right.* So you say, *Take care.* Which means, *Can you please manage to get a basic enough hold of yourself so that I won't have to spend my own dwindling time on earth feeling guilty and uneasy about you.* So I can forget about everything else in the day to day, except the increasingly dear immediates. Food. Warmth. Sleep.

The man who lives with me.

We stopped seeing Artie Schumann. Neil's righted himself, is the way I see it. I'm still not sure how it happened. Though I know it began—something shifted—the night we drove home from the baptism, as I came to call it, in the Hilton pool.

☙

I INSISTED on driving; he didn't argue. I'd brought along my night-driving glasses, thank goodness—helpful for spotting bicyclists, reading street signs, the church marquee: GREAT MUSIC, RELEVANT MESSAGES. Poor church, trying harder and harder. Bumper stickers. ABUNDANCE IS EVERYWHERE. DIE TAILGATER SCUM. They take on a meta-life of their own, slogans like alien melodies, and my lips curved up catching sight of them. PROUD TO BE VEGAN. I LOVE MY BULLDOG. NAVY MOM. Neil sat next to me, in a pink sweat suit of Addie's, looking straight ahead. It was the only thing she and Tilda could dig up for him from their luggage, after he'd toweled down in Tilda's hotel bathroom. It fit him comically, far too short for his phone-pole arms and legs, a Hilton towel slung around his shoulders like a toddler's superhero cape. He wore his wet loafers, which squeaked as he walked. I said nothing though his costume would, under other circumstances, have been uproarious. We slunk out the service door to the parking lot to avoid being seen (though by then it was thoroughly dark), maneuvering among the motorcycles of the guests still partying, Neil's soaked things bundled in a plastic garbage bag donated by the hotel's night staff. As I drove he sat silent—chilled, I knew, because he shivered a bit under his superhero towel, though I blasted the car's heater. This worried me; he's tough as a dray horse, almost never sick, but chills can bring him down. I drove with care under a starless sky, the moon a gauzed white fruit someone had carved a slice from. Once we stepped inside I pushed the thermostat all the way up and directed him to strip.

While he peeled off the pink sweat suit, I ran the bath as hot as I knew he could stand. I poured in a long dose of Epsom salts, filled the tub halfway. He's so tall he always has to crouch a little to enter the sliding-glass frame that runs the length of the tub. I watched him fold himself into the water, his mass displacing it to nearly the tub's edge, knees and shins sticking up; he leaned back, shut his eyes, and sighed: a sigh of pure, absolute relinquishing. I still believe that something literally escaped him then, some obdurate idea. Flew out from his person on that emptying sigh, like a trapped ghost hitching a ride.

I folded an old towel and tucked it behind his head. I soaked a washcloth in the steaming water, wrung it and laid it over his face. He didn't move.

"That okay?"

"Ymmph."

Outside, the sky had filled and a wind risen. Rain pebbled the window glass. The bamboo wind-chimes swung from the backyard maple, banging out their Balinese scale, up and down, up and down.

He lay still in the high water, all knees, shoulders. From time to time I'd hear a small *splish* as he dipped the washcloth to re-soak it and press it to his face. The old forced-air heater had whooshed on, warming the bathroom fast, and I felt satisfied he would cook out whatever threatened him.

I went to the bedroom, took off my clothes, slipped on my terry robe. Padded to the kitchen, filled the electric kettle, fetched the tea. After I'd made us each a cup I could hear him lifting himself slowly from the tub, a noisy, reverse-displacement, waterfall sound. I found a clean, heavy towel and rubbed him everywhere, his skin pink, every freckle and mole familiar. I wrapped him in his fleece robe, blue and black plaid—remembered buying that robe for him for Christmas; he'd picked it out. I've harrassed him so over the years about washing the robe more often; he feigns hurt when I insist it's overripe. Yet alone, tucking it into the washing machine like the plush hide of a big blue lion, I've chastised myself: If anything were to happen to him I'd sleep with that robe, bury my face in its musk.

I led him to bed, threw back the covers, placed his tea on the nightstand. Then I went to bathe myself.

When I came back, towel-wrapped, pink and damp, he was on his back, still in his robe, not having bothered to pull up the covers (the house thoroughly warm by then). Without a word he opened the robe, and his arms. I doffed the towel and lay full-length on top of him, kissed his chest and neck and shoulders, cheeks and chin, mouth. Sighed. Both of us smelled like Dove soap. We looked at each other.

"I should make soup, night like this," he said. "Eh?"

Sly parentheses around his lips, eyes lit with a familiar tenderness.

I was so relieved I could've wept. He was back somehow, Neil again. For some reason I'd got him back. Why, I swear I'm still not sure, and may never be. Did the pool-dunking waken him to something, or my caring for him afterward, the soak in the tub? Had his initial grief, formed as anger, run its course?

Perhaps he finally understood that I did not wish Mike dead.

Nothing's ruled out. Maybe I should expect a different form of grief next, a second shoe. Or a reprise of the first. He could certainly disappear on me again. That hard face I so dread may revisit. *Malaise invaded; malaise can return.* But for the time being, I'd shut up. Some things you learn to shut up about.

Others you stumble forward, take a chance on.

"Will it be okay," I whispered, "if I put just the wee-est little bit of hot sauce in my portion?"

He pushed my hair behind my ear. "Of ahll the gin joints in ahll the toownes in ahll the werrld—"

Then he rolled us over so that I lay beneath him, my arms around his neck, and his open robe was our tent.

◦◦◦

ARTIE HAD nodded, squinting and cheerful, when we alerted him the following week we'd not be returning anytime soon. We'd explained we felt better—Neil felt better. I was practicing being more mindful, I said, checking what he wanted, needed. He would do the same with me. For me.

"Awareness of the plate," I'd said, catching Neil's eye.

Artie squinted.

We would work at it more consciously. Work included play. We'd schedule fallow time for me, detox time between social gigs. I'd look for things we might enjoy doing. (I'd try.) Neil would eat slower. (He'd try.) The prosaic compromises. We knew it was foolish—Artie had pointed this out—to dump baby with bathwater when, in Artie's words, "there is so much you agree on!"

He'd stood and shaken our hands like a tour guide. "Come back every six months if you want! For a tune-up! And send books, send books!" he'd called to me as we left.

⌘

IN MY ear Tilda too sounds merry—or at least, giving her best depiction of it. "Oh yeah, just fine, doing fine."

A pause.

"Neil's not around, I gather?"

"Sorry, he's at the gym. He always goes about this time on weekends."

A pause. I know it cheeses her off he's not here. She'd infinitely rather talk to him.

"Yeah, well. Give him my best, then. Appreciated those e-mails, Rae; I can always tell it's you, recognize that breathy voice of yours."

I look at the receiver in my hand.

Breathy.

Breathy?

Never make a writer angry, Tilda.

Out the window the robins laugh and wheel. In an hour I'll find a dead one at the foot of the back steps, breast up, unmolested, unmarked, head turned slightly away, milky eyes half-closed. I forget how bitter, how furious the natural struggle is out there, even just outside the mellow confines of the house. Perhaps a midair collision, a fatal drunken tumble. Perhaps an attack by a predator. Maybe the bird's system chose the preceding minute to click off, some internal toggle, handsome and robust though the creature will look. I'll wrap it gently in a paper towel—aware how terrified it would have been minutes ago, alive, to be held this way in a human hand—humbled by its perfect heft, flawless colors and feathering, not made or controlled by any man. I'll carry it to the trash bin, murmuring, *I'm sorry*.

I go to the message machine, press the playback button. When Tilda's recorded "Yo, sweeties!" begins, I punch the delete button, hard.

"End of final message," states the machine's genial voice. Courteous, alert, vacant. That same voice tells you the location of the emergency exits, the window number of the available teller at the Department of Motor Vehicles.

Maybe I'll tell Neil later about Tilda's call.

But I won't tell him about the ashes. I will gamble that she won't make the offer a second time, or bring it up again.

I will be right.

I watch the mailbox for a few weeks. No ashes ever arrive.

*I*t's late spring that prompts my remembering, many springs since the story of Mike and Tilda. Evenings, obeying the laws of spring, settle imperceptibly, soft and temperate. And Neil has fallen asleep in front of the television.

I've been reading in bed, wander out of the bedroom to tell him something, and find him there. The lamp on the glass table throws butterscotch light over his empty brandy snifter, over the framed photos beyond his shoulder and beyond them, to the shelf where he's arranged the latest set of little thank-you carvings; in the dim light they resemble findings from an anthropological dig, color and form of animal crackers.

Smells of tonight's dinner still sift through the house: couscous, chicken in Cuban mojito sauce. For dessert we peeled blood oranges. Neil decided some time back we should eat a bit further down the food chain: better for us, for the retirees' budget, the nature of things. Brandy doesn't yet appear to figure anywhere in the new asceticism.

Besides that, though, days tick along, as Neil puts it. Their rhythm has come to define us. Certain cups are used to make morning coffee. The potted bougainvillea is hauled inside when frost threatens. Every Christmas the small tree perches on the same red terry bathmat, no matter what. Eccentricities, routines— admitted to no one but each other—comfort us as deeply and illogically as a dog's pocked chew toy.

In ways, Neil says, he has become his late father, unable to resist the thick down-spiralling pull of sleep after a meal.

He snores away, slumped against the couch back, chin tipped down, hands carefully laced over his sternum. He could be praying, or dozing through a sermon or transcontinental flight. Except his crossed feet are bare—still beautiful, those feet, long, articulated toes and tendons like feet in Renaissance paintings. The television screams, frantic to rouse him—exercise equipment, tequila, Jacuzzi tubs, bail bonds.

I sit down beside him, click off the television. Place my hand on his blue-jeaned knee, his sweatered arm.

"Neilly. Neil. Sweetheart."

Rolling, liquid snores. The kind of sleep we call *bottom of the sea*. It's a purity, that sleep. Like drowning in cream.

I watch his chest rise, fall. I lean closer and breathe in. Vanilla. I sit back, lean against the couch beside him, exhale a long breath.

Whoever thinks, in the moment of it, I wonder, *Now we are ending?*

Oh, few. Even those of us who flow faster toward it. Especially not the young, their animal life beating under their skins, who can't yet imagine any ends at all except in video games or digital films, hulky droids spurting computer graphics blood. Daily confrontations don't yet signify for them: the little clock by the bed, the gray dawn, the cold stars.

Odds are good he'll go before me, I know. Actuarial odds. The drinking, the cigars. I've worried about it since we met, and he's teased me, maybe rightfully, about morbidity.

On the other hand, life—death—tend to surprise, by definition.

His arm in its waffle-weave cotton sleeve, warm and calm beneath my hand. His face and body softened, deep. Beside him on the glass table stands an echo-image of his sleeping face, but awake and beaming in black and white—a photo of the two of us, one of many. Leaning into each other. Ichabod and Carmen. I had longer hair then; no white had yet shown in it. Arms folded across my chest as if to say, *Yeah, this is us. Wanna make something of it?* If we'd been standing back to back in the shot we'd resemble a vaudeville dance poster.

Of dance, I finally convinced him. Signed us up for lessons. Ballroom. "Where'd this come from?" he'd asked, eyeing me when I showed him the flyer; his amusement so pointed that for a moment I almost regressed into anger. But I could see he was pleased, and that counted. Something for another part of our brains, my idea for once. And we won't act murderous or lean away from each other, like the TV vampires. A good project for mild nights. Days are warmer and sweeter, awash in birdsong— great fountains of it, like they'd waited all their lives for these mornings. New buds showing early this year, shiny little battalions, as if someone has called them out from hiding with a secret whistle: wine-colored bullets opening to green on the Japanese maple, green-to-white on the plum, cranberry-stained pink on the peach. Another spring.

I write, he reads. We walk around the lake at the park. Petals like pastel confetti floating there, floating over town, eddying in the streets. Their fragrances collide in your nostrils—honey, lilac, vine jasmine, freesia, lemon blossom, hosts of others whose names I've never bothered to learn.

You take your amazement where you find it.

In dreams, as well. Traces of last night's still drag at my blood. We were traveling on a bus, an outing. Old friends, long ago lovers, handsome architecture, shining landscape; air a pewter sheen. The crowd of us stopped at a movie house, sat in the first row fussing and whispering; I seem to remember spilling my paper cup of concession drink, but it wasn't sticky; nobody minded. We left as a group, re-boarded the bus, for some reason dressed in bathrobes, pajamas. We reached a campsite; people began to unpack and set up. Neil was there, and there was Mike—whole and hearty again, a grinning Sinbad—and all the old dinner party crew, many of them gone now. I stood near each by turns, arm around a shoulder or neck. Provisions appeared—hunks of expensive gold cheese with a dark, aged rind, superb and plentiful; people held chunks in their hands, milling, grinning, a tribe in the giddiest sense, music, shouting, jokes. And soon a line of arm-linked dancers began snaking Greek-style through the setting. In ragged, wavelike motion they moved up an embankment toward a grass-covered ridge: a dancing line of laughing friends in their pajamas, people I'd known, people from our time, Neil's and mine. I woke certain that something had been shown to me, something I must find a way, at all costs, to remember.

Who remains, who's pending—I see us all gliding smoothly, along the Niagara River. Cooling mist, algal smells, rippling strings of moss; the roar increasing so subtly you don't notice till it's upon you. Things going in one direction, ending badly, this isn't news. The only news left is how, what *kind* of badly. We stalk past one another on the street, we guide the car through the intersection, raise our glasses and say *cheers* and *cin cin* and *to us*, our faces scheduled to dessicate like trampled leaves, be part of someone's dreams awhile, finally nothing but the silent movement of air, stars, matter.

But not yet. Thank stars, thank matter.

We don't have to end just yet.

I watch my sleeping husband, his snores gentling in and out: small waves washing pebbles. And I remember him weeping for Mike, all those years ago.

We seldom speak of it anymore. It took awhile to *sort*, as Neil would say. More than a cartoon, a circus strongman or petty gangster, more than a horny goat—Mike was an old-fashioned gondolier, the boatman who sings as he guides his craft, working his pole through the filthy waters of life, singing in full throat without shame, as if his heart might burst for beauty. Mike had never asked for love but simply been love itself, which asked nothing. You can't discount that, whatever other trouble it made. I guess that's what Tilda could not bear in the end, perhaps quite understandably.

Neil finally persuaded the city and the downtown merchants, after a year or two of pestering, to imbed an engraved brass plaque in the sidewalk where Finny Business had stood. (The space is leased now by an optometrist; its front windows fitted with posters of chiseled models, men and women wearing designer eyeglasses; their gazes cool and shrewd, as if seeing into the secret hearts of things). The plaque's print is smaller than Neil wanted. Shiny, though. Catches light, like a golden tooth in a gray mouth. Groups of tourists still stop to study it. They can even look it up in the guidebook the Chamber of Commerce publishes—which we remind each other would have given Mike the biggest, fattest kick. I can see him inflating all over, if he'd known. MICHAEL FIELD SPENDER, BUSINESSMAN AND NATURALIST, 1950–2008. Neil made me promise to keep quiet, didn't want it known that he paid for most of the plaque's cost. Now, few are alive to whom it would make any difference.

For Tilda, no plaque. How might such a marker read, I used to wonder. After a time—as with so very much else—I put the question away. Something for larger minds than mine to solve, some faraway day.

"Sweetheart." I stroke his shoulder, his warm cheek.

"Neilly, wake up. Wake up, sweetheart, so we can get you to bed."

The patient house waits in the night.

The windows can stay open wider now. In a month or so the crickets will start, a sound like small, winking lights.